"Mikala." His voice was husky, almost raw.

She knew what he wanted. But he wouldn't take it, not unless she gave the signal she was willing. They both remembered prom night. They both remembered the other kisses they'd shared. She could see the need in his eyes, feel it in the tension that crackled in the air between them.

She leaned toward him, ever so slightly. His arm came around her. When she turned toward him, her leg brushed his. His face was so close, his lips simply a whisper away.

She could still pull back. She didn't have to let this happen. But she suddenly wanted Dawson's kiss more than she'd ever wanted anything in her life.

Dear Reader,

I remember the first time a boy asked me to dance, the color and softness of his sweater, the step into a closeness I'd never experienced before. Becoming lost in the music while being held is an experience like no other.

My heroine, Mikala, danced with Dawson at her prom and the night of the reunion. Music has become her life. A music therapist, Mikala helps children who need her. Dawson's son needs her. Although she and Dawson haven't seen each other for fifteen years, their high school reunion brings back the past—the night Dawson became her white knight. Mikala falls deeply in love with him, but can the music in her heart help him heal his own past hurts so they can find a future together?

The CEO's Unexpected Proposal is the third book in my Reunion Brides series. I hope this romance touches your heart the way it touched mine.

All my best,

Karen Rose Smith

THE CEO'S
UNEXPECTED
PROPOSAL

KAREN ROSE SMITH

HARLEQUIN®
entertain, enrich, inspire™

Recycling programs
for this product may
not exist in your area.

ISBN-13: 978-0-373-65683-7

THE CEO'S UNEXPECTED PROPOSAL

www.Harlequin.com

Printed in U.S.A.

KAREN ROSE SMITH

is an award-winning, bestselling novelist of over seventy published romances. Her latest series, Reunion Brides, is set near Flagstaff, Arizona, in Miners Bluff, the fictional town she created. After visiting Flagstaff, the Grand Canyon and Sedona, she felt that the scenery was so awe-inspiring that she had to set books there. When not writing, she likes to garden, growing herbs, vegetables and flowers. She lives with her husband—her college sweetheart—and their two cats in Pennsylvania. Readers may email her through her website at www.karenrosesmith.com, follow her on Facebook or Twitter @karenrosesmith, or write to her at P.O. Box 1545, Hanover, PA 17331.

In memory of my mother, Romaine Arcuri Cacciola, who gave me my love of music. I miss you.

Prologue

July
Fifteenth Year High School Reunion

Her heart racing, Mikala Conti watched as Dawson Barrett crossed the cafeteria floor and extended his hand.

"Would you like to dance?"

She hadn't seen him for fifteen years. The blue-and-yellow streamers decorating the ceiling and the spinning silver mirror ball faded away as she remembered catching glimpses of him in this cafeteria so many years ago. Memories sifted around her, like the reflective silver light. One stood out—prom night—and the way Dawson had rescued her from a terrible situation.

"It's been a long time," she said, shaking off the flash from the past as she took his hand and rose to her feet.

He guided her a short distance away to a free spot on the tiled floor and took her into his arms.

Mikala felt breathless—sort of light-headed—and she knew she had to get a grip. She wasn't like this. She was never giddy or impulsive or even daring. But as Dawson's hand skimmed across her back under her long, wavy black hair, as it came to rest on the silky fabric of her sedate yet dressy black dress, she couldn't seem to control any of her body's reactions.

He seemed to enjoy the moment, too. When she gazed up into his eyes she remembered the boy he'd been and realized what an absolutely sexy man he'd become. They danced together as if they had done it more than once before. His green eyes didn't reflect all the years between then and now. They reflected a bond they'd once had.

But then he said—

"I didn't come tonight just for old times' sake. I needed to talk to you. I know you're a music therapist. My son needs your help. Will you consider taking him on as a patient?"

Remembering again the night of her prom, Mikala knew she'd do anything she could to help Dawson.

For old times' sake.

Chapter One

January

Mikala checked the music-note-shaped wall clock, her heart pounding faster with each passing minute. Her studio, a two-room cabinlike structure in the backyard of the Purple Pansy Bed-and-Breakfast, was her second home. Growing up, she'd wrapped herself in music—listening to it, playing it, getting lost in the emotion of it—whenever life got complicated.

Now Dawson Barrett wanted her to use music to help his son.

Last summer they'd reconnected at their high school reunion. Then before Christmas Dawson had called and confirmed he'd be moving back to Miners Bluff and putting Luke under her care.

The cabin's chiming doorbell melodically announced Dawson's arrival. He'd said he'd be here at one-thirty, and it was one-thirty on the dot. She'd dressed with more care than usual, wearing a deep purple cowl-neck sweater over gray slacks. Smoothing her hands down over her hips, she took a deep breath and pushed her long, black hair over one shoulder.

When she opened the door, the January wind swept in. Right away she noticed the deep lines around Dawson's eyes, a furrow in his brow and fatigue on his face. His sandy brown hair was windswept and his leather jacket was zipped tight against the cold.

Their dance last summer was vivid in her mind—the way he'd held her, the way her heart had fluttered madly. Also still vivid were memories that went farther back—prom night, how he'd given her the ability to dream.

But then he'd left without a word. And all these years she'd wondered about him and the life he'd found, even though she'd heard rumors that he'd been widowed, was a wealthy CEO and a success in the field of construction.

"Come in!" She motioned to the office area of her studio, thinking Dawson looked as if he needed to get warm.

"I cut it a little close." He gave her one of those smiles that had always affected something deep inside of her. "You said on the phone you had an appointment to meet with the principal at the elementary school at three-thirty."

"I do, and none too soon."

She felt an urgency about Dawson now that hadn't been in his voice when they'd spoken before. "Did something happen?"

"Luke tried to run away."

"Oh, Dawson. Let's sit."

Besides her mahogany desk, there was a cranberry-colored corduroy love seat and two camel leather club chairs. They gravitated to the love seat as Dawson unzipped his jacket and shrugged out of it. She couldn't help but notice the breadth of his shoulders in his navy sweater, the way his jeans hugged his slim hips and long legs.

This was Dawson, she told herself sternly. He was a friend who needed her help.

Memories from high school came rushing back—poring over algebra in the library with him, catching a ride home in his yellow Mustang, talking with their friends around the kitchen table at the B and B the night of the prom.

Shoving any thoughts but those of his ten-year-old son aside, she suggested, "Tell me what happened."

He tossed his jacket over a chair and lowered himself to the love seat beside her. After taking in his surroundings in a glance, peering into the music room with its sofa, folding chairs, instruments—the piano front and center—Dawson brought his gaze back to hers. "Luke's class has been exploring the benefits of computers as far as exchanging information with other schools. They partnered with a school in Kentucky and Luke made an online friend. When he tried to run away, he almost hopped a bus to Kentucky where Jared lives."

She could hardly imagine the scare Dawson had experienced with Luke trying to run away. Longing to be a parent herself, the past few years she'd considered registering with an adoption agency. If she was a mom, the idea of a child being lost out in the world would be terrifying.

Dawson raked his hand through his hair. "I'd been working in my home office, and I didn't even know he was gone. Another half hour and he would have been on that bus."

"What exactly is going on?" She knew the basics. She'd received the evaluation and notes from Luke's two previous therapists, who hadn't been able to make headway with him. Dawson's wife had died in an automobile accident and Luke had been in the car with her. Yet he didn't remember the day of the accident *or* the accident. Most of all, he refused to cooperate with any attempt to form the trust-bond so necessary to counselor-client success. Mikala knew about losing a mom, though her circumstances had been very different from Luke's. No child got over that loss easily.

"Bottom line, he's unhappy," Dawson said. "He's fighting at school. He hardly talks to me. I think he feels pressured to remember what happened and believes I expect him to. I only want him to remember if it will help him."

Mikala thought about that. "It might help. It could hurt. We won't know until I get to know him a bit."

After a few beats of silence Dawson admitted, "For the first time since I started my business, I'm going to be hands-off for a while. Luke is my main concern. My dad's my right-hand man and he'll stay in Phoenix overseeing the company. I have other good people there, too. I won't be working like I used to."

"Long days to make the business thrive?" Through Miners Bluff's gossip mills, she'd heard Dawson's contracting company had found success when other companies couldn't. But that was no consolation now. She could see regrets in his green eyes and couldn't figure out exactly what they were from. She needed to know about his regrets if she was going to help his son. Some of them might have touched Luke.

"What's bothering you *most?*" she prompted, hoping Dawson would be open with her so she *could* help.

"Most?" he asked with a wry grin that wasn't really a grin. "I've worked sixteen-hour days for as long as I can remember. Not as many since Kelly died, but enough. Maybe that made Luke's problem worse."

Mikala's radar went on alert at his regretful tone. When she'd known Dawson in high school, she'd not only wanted to be around him because he was sexy. She'd loved spending time with him because he was kind and respectful and never took advantage of any of his friends. Were his regrets tied into his success… or his marriage? Years of practice had her wait in silence for Dawson to continue.

"For years I thought Kelly and I were happy," he finally said. "As my business grew, we moved to a bigger house, and when Luke was ready, enrolled him in a private school. I wasn't home much, but when I was, I thought everything was okay. But after Luke started school, Kelly began to change."

Dawson broke eye contact. "Maybe none of this matters. My main concerns are Luke's fighting, his not getting along in school, his grades plummeting. But most of all his general attitude. I just need to know how to talk to him…how to get through to him."

Before Mikala could stop herself, she covered Dawson's hand with hers. To her surprise, the contact was electric. She glimpsed a startled look in his eyes, too, and she pulled her hand back quickly.

"It *all* matters, Dawson. Children are sponges. They soak in their surroundings, everything they hear, everything they see and even the feelings swirling around them. So whether you think something's important or not, it doesn't hurt to tell me."

Quickly Dawson swung his gaze back to her, studying her face. Then he rubbed his forehead. "Okay." After a few pensive moments, he blew out a breath. "Kelly and I married because she was pregnant. And…" He hesitated. "She didn't go back to work after Luke was born. I was making serious money then, so her working didn't matter. We decided not to hire a nanny. But once Luke started school, she seemed to want her freedom more…to work out, attend clubs, join charity groups. I think she came to resent the fact she was the one who had most of the responsibility for Luke."

When Dawson stopped, she had the feeling there was something he wasn't telling her. But she didn't halt the flow of his thoughts. "I made the point of coming home early now and then to be there when Luke got off the bus. He seemed happy and I was always grateful for that."

Dawson went silent again, then continued, "That December Luke had the day off for teacher in-service. A babysitter was supposed to watch him so Kelly could go holiday shopping in Flagstaff and stay overnight. At the last minute the babysitter canceled, and Kelly couldn't reach me. I was on a job site and my phone went to voice mail. So she left me a message that she was taking Luke with her."

Mikala watched as Dawson's face became set, his shoulders more square. He seemed to want to distance himself from the memory. His voice dropped to a far-away monotone. "There was ice on the road. She went off the side of a deep shoulder, the car rolled and hit a tree. She wasn't wearing a seatbelt…she was killed on impact."

Dawson cleared his throat, pain all too evident in his expression.

Mikala said gently, "Take your time."

One of his hands balled into a fist. "I lost Kelly, but I was so grateful Luke survived. He was in the hospital for a week, recovering from a concussion and internal injuries. It was touch-and-go for two days and when he woke up, he didn't remember anything that had happened the day of the accident or that night. I took him to therapists and he wouldn't talk to them. He withdrew even more. *I* can't get through to him. My dad can't, either. When I found him at the bus station, he cried and screamed that he didn't want to go home."

Mikala could only guess what that had done to Dawson—how it had hurt him more deeply than he could say.

"I don't know what to do for him," he said in a low voice, as if the admission cost him. "When I found out you were a music therapist who came highly recommended, I came to the reunion believing the idea of you treating Luke seemed to be the best one because Luke loves music. He's taken piano lessons since he was seven. And I think Miners Bluff will be good for us both."

When she and Dawson had danced together at the reunion, an old attraction to him had tugged at her.

But it had no place here. Dawson's life was in turmoil and his son was his priority and would be hers, too.

Still, as their gazes held, the room seemed to shake a little. Yet Dawson was counting on her as a friend who could help his son. She would assist any child in this situation.

"I'll do my best to help put Luke on a healthy emotional path. I can't tell you I'm going to solve anything, Dawson, but I can at least try to get the two of you talking again."

A light rap on the door startled them, and Mikala knew it must be her Aunt Anna. She didn't have her in-session sign up. But if she didn't answer the knock, her aunt would go about her business, knowing Mikala couldn't be interrupted.

Glancing at Dawson's face, she could see he hadn't wanted to revisit the past, but he'd done it for his son's sake. She assured him, "I don't have to answer that."

"Go ahead," he said with a small smile and she could see he was glad for the break.

When she stood, her arm brushed Dawson's shoulder. Again there was a quick meeting of their gazes, but neither said anything. She felt totally unsettled and was glad to open the door again and feel the cold breeze.

Her Aunt Anna smiled at her. "I saw the car, but your sign wasn't turned around so I thought—"

"It's okay. Come on in. Dawson Barrett's here." She didn't say more. If Dawson wanted her aunt to know anything else, he would tell her.

Her aunt's wavy, steel-gray hair attractively framed her face. She was wearing a jogging suit with a down jacket and her favorite pair of sneakers. Mikala's heart contracted with love for this woman who had raised her. She owed her aunt more than she could ever repay and she loved her dearly.

Dawson stood and came forward, hand extended.

"Hello, Ms. Conti. It's good to see you again."

Aunt Anna never stood on ceremony. She wrapped her arms around Dawson for a hug. "Don't give me that 'Ms. Conti' baloney. You called me Aunt Anna when you were a teenager. You can still call me that." She stood back to take a better look at him. "Mikala told me you were at the reunion. She's never forgotten you, you know. You were her white knight at the prom."

Mikala wanted to crawl under the love seat, but Dawson chuckled. "I don't know how much of a white knight I was."

His green gaze rested on Mikala and she remembered everything about that night in vivid detail—her torn dress, the date who had tried to maul her in the back of his car, Dawson coming to her rescue when she'd called out. Even more than all that, she remembered Dawson's gentle kiss on her forehead after he'd taken her home. She'd told her aunt what had happened.

After what seemed like an excruciatingly long time, Dawson turned back to Anna. "Did Mikala tell you I'm moving back to Miners Bluff?"

"No, she didn't." Anna waited for him to explain.

"I have a ten-year-old son. My wife died and he's having a hard time. So I thought moving back here, giving him roots in a smaller community might help. Mikala's skill as a music therapist is well-known. She's going to spend some time with him."

"Well, if anyone can help him get settled again, I'm sure she can. Is your son with you?"

"No, not yet. I came up today to meet with Mikala, to see the school and register him, to stay over and re-familiarize myself with what's here. I'll bring Luke up to Miners Bluff in a couple of weeks when his term in Phoenix ends."

"I see." Anna paused, looked at Mikala and then asked Dawson, "Do you have a place to stay tonight… or when you move back?"

"Not yet. I was going to check into a motel and look for something temporary until I find a house. I'm going to check around before I return to Phoenix."

"If I could make a suggestion," Anna offered.

"I'm open to suggestions," Dawson responded with that smile that could disarm anyone. He'd always been an easy conversationalist. As senior class president and a basketball star, he'd had his pick of girls to date. Yet his circle of friends had been most important to him.

"January isn't a prime tourist month in Miners Bluff," Anna explained wryly. "So the bed-and-break-fast has two suites vacant, one on the first floor with one bedroom and one on the third with two bedrooms. You could have your pick. For tonight and for when you return. I'd even give you a weekly rate since you don't know how long you'd need to stay."

"Aunt Anna, Dawson might want something…dif-ferent than the B and B."

Actually, Dawson looked relieved. "No, I think the Purple Pansy might be perfect. Convenient for tonight. And just right for me and Luke. Staying here could be good for him. That is, if your biscotti and pie are part of the deal."

Anna laughed. "You drive a hard bargain. But biscotti are always in the jar and I make pies twice a week. I never know who will drop in, or if I'll get a last-minute reservation."

"Could I take a look at the suites now?" Dawson asked.

"Well…" Anna drawled. "I have a meeting in town. But Mikala could show them to you."

Her aunt hadn't mentioned a meeting that morning when they'd spoken. She wasn't trying to play match-maker, was she? Because Dawson wasn't ready for that. She wasn't sure she was, either—or would ever be.

Dawson was looking at her expectantly.

"Sure, I can show them to you. We should have enough time before your appointment."

Mikala took her wool jacket from the coatrack be-hind the door, slipped it on and buttoned it up to the neck even though they weren't walking very far. For some reason she felt as if she needed all of her defenses buttoned into place around Dawson. Which made no sense. Her dreams of attracting someone like Daw-son had died a long time ago. She knew she wasn't sexy. She knew loving brought heartache and doubled a woman's insecurities.

In high school Dawson's casual good looks had gotten him dates with all the popular girls and his souped-up Mustang had made him the envy of most of the guys. Dawson had been popular and cool. Play-ing basketball and being able to talk to anyone had helped that image.

She, on the other hand, had been mostly quiet and introspective.

Locking up the high school memories in a tight box, she led Dawson out the door and up the flagstone path to the Purple Pansy, not only a well-liked B and B on the northern Arizona tourist route, but her home for all of her thirty-three years. Her aunt had run the B and B since before Mikala was born in addition to giving piano lessons, taking in typing for a temp agency and working as a receptionist on and off. Anna had worked hard to keep a roof over their heads, good food on the table and laughter in the kitchen. Mikala knew she could never repay her aunt for raising her when her mother had left and hardly looked back.

"There's snow in the air," Dawson remarked, as they walked along the path profuse with flowers in summer and fall, now barren with the winter cold.

Glancing over at Dawson, she had to look up. She wasn't short. She was a good five-eight. "Very different from Phoenix."

"Maybe I can coax Luke outdoors more here and involve him in winter sports. He spends too much time cooped up in his room. Cactus and heat don't help."

"Does he have a specific reason for fighting the move?" No one particularly liked change, but children could be more resilient than adults.

"He's protesting in part because my dad's staying there. And, of course, Phoenix is the only home he knows. It's where we were a family. Where he had his mom."

Mikala saw the sadness in Dawson's eyes when he spoke of his deceased wife. But she sensed he was hurting more for Luke than himself. Was she right about that? Had Dawson's marriage been less than he'd expected it to be? Had an unplanned pregnancy made it rocky from the start?

On the patio of the B and B, Dawson looked around

at the sycamores and pines, Moonshadow Mountain and Feather Peak in the distance.

"It's just as I remembered it."

There was nostalgia in his voice and she wondered exactly what he was remembering.

When they stepped into the kitchen, Mikala caught the scent of vanilla and lavender. The whole house seemed to have that scent, except when she or her aunt were baking. Then cinnamon and fruit smells filled every nook and cranny.

There was surprise in Dawson's voice when he said, "*This* changed."

The house was about a hundred years old and well-maintained. Overall, it had an old-fashioned air, with bronze sconces on walls that resembled oil lamps, ceiling lights with chandelier bulbs and wallpaper with tiny purple and yellow flowers. However, the kitchen had seen a major overhaul.

Glancing around, Mikala smiled. "Stainless steel moved in so I guess it's more modern. We have a new counter and floor, too. But some things are still the same."

Dawson's gaze passed over the oak clock above the sink, the railing above the cupboards holding Hummel figurines, the maple table and chairs that were antiques now.

"She still has the purple pansy curtains." He couldn't keep the amusement from his voice.

"Yes, she does. They're fairly new, though, the old ones had faded."

"This still feels…homey," Dawson mused, and Mikala had to wonder if his house didn't.

Decisive again, he motioned down the hall. "Let's

look at the third-floor suite. Two bedrooms would be better to give both Luke and I some privacy."

As they walked down the hall, Mikala tried to avoid thinking about the fact that if Dawson took the third-floor suite, *she'd* be on the second floor. Her quarters and her aunt's were there. Having Dawson under the same roof gave her stomach an upside-down kind of feeling.

The carpet runner on the stairs quieted their footsteps. As they climbed the second flight, she asked him, "How much will you be bringing with you?"

"Just enough to make Luke comfortable. I'll have his bedroom furniture and the piano trucked up here when we're ready, but the rest of it I'm going to leave at the house. The market is picking up there, and with everything priced right, I'm hoping a furnished house will sell quickly. If Luke and I are starting a new life, it will be better that way."

"You might ask him if there's anything else he wants to keep. Baggage is one thing, Dawson, but memories are another. You don't want to tear him away from *everything* he knows. He could be fighting the move because he feels that's what you're doing."

At the landing now, Dawson looked troubled. "I hope I'm not making a mistake. But nothing is working for Luke in Phoenix."

"What's your gut telling you?" Mikala asked, as they stood at the door to the third-floor suite, close enough to share confidences and remember friendship that might have been more. If only—

If only Dawson's family hadn't moved away, whatever the reason.

"My gut's telling me this is right."

"Then maybe I can help him marry the past with the present."

The word *marry* seemed to hang between them and she wondered why she'd chosen that word. To remind herself Dawson had been married? That even after two years he might still be grieving? That nothing could come of any attraction she might feel? That *she* didn't trust that anyone would stay and not leave, especially a man...especially someone she loved? She'd been left behind more than once and she wouldn't let it happen again. The memory of Alan Taylor telling her he'd fallen for someone else still stung...still hurt...bringing back a feeling of inadequacy she'd fought against since she was a teenager.

Mikala took a key ring from her pocket. It jangled as she poked an old-fashioned key into the door and turned the lock. The solid wood door swung open. She and Dawson stepped inside to a sitting room where braided rugs in hunter green and navy dotted the floor. The navy leather couch was accompanied by a green and blue plaid chair.

Mikala switched on a multi-colored Tiffany lamp so Dawson could see there was a small kitchen area with a microwave, two-burner stove and a table for two. Yellow curtains and placemats brightened up the small space.

As Dawson assessed the suite, Mikala crossed the room to a short hall. She opened one door to reveal a nice-sized bedroom with a hand-carved oak bed and dresser. A handmade quilt with navy, red, green and yellow patches stretched across the bed. The second bedroom, slightly smaller with a slanted ceiling, had an oak washstand with mirror, a shorter dresser and a double bed. Light poured in the double-hung windows, splashing over the green-and-tan spread.

"This is perfect," Dawson decided. "I think Luke and I will both feel comfortable here." He took a check-book from his inside jacket pocket. "I should give your aunt a deposit."

Automatically Mikala's hand closed over his. "No, don't worry about that. She'll settle up with you when the time comes."

Time seemed suspended for a moment as she could feel the heat of his hand under hers. He didn't move and neither did she. Then she realized she should let go. She shouldn't be touching him.

Hurriedly she released her fingers from his and dropped her hand to her side. But Dawson still seemed frozen in place. He studied her, maybe searching for the girl she'd once been, a scared lost teenager not knowing exactly who she was or where she belonged.

Before she could square her shoulders and tell him she was somebody very different now, he took her back fifteen years by gently grazing his thumb over her cheek. "When we were in high school—" He suddenly stopped, dropping his hand to his side.

"What?" she urged him, believing it was somehow important that he went on.

"I was going to ask you to the prom."

Knowing the value of silence, she waited.

"But too much was going on at home. Then someone else asked you instead."

Oh, yes. Carson Simmons had asked her to the prom and she'd gone with him because he'd been a football player, one of the in-crowd, someone who lots of girls wanted to go out with. But she'd found out that night why he didn't seem to date anyone more than twice. She'd found out the hard way that some boys wanted to do more than talk and couldn't—wouldn't—take no for an answer.

"After I brought you home that night," Dawson added, "I was going to call you."

This time she couldn't keep quiet. "But you didn't."

"All hell broke loose at home and things got…complicated." Their gazes locked until he said, "A little bit like now."

As if the moment had been much too intense for both of them, he slipped his checkbook back into his jacket pocket then checked his watch. "I'd better go."

"I spend some of my time at the elementary school working with students who need help with communication and behavioral issues. Do you want me to go with you? I can show you around before your meeting with the principal."

As soon as she offered, she wasn't sure she should have…because Dawson was looking at her the same way he had the night of their prom.

"I'd like that," he responded huskily.

At that moment, Mikala knew she had to bury whatever feelings she'd once had for Dawson so she could help his son.

That was the professional road to take…the one she *must* take.

Chapter Two

As Dawson and Mikala signed in at the office of Miners Bluff's elementary school, he dropped the keys to his SUV in his pocket and glanced at her. She'd changed a lot since high school. He'd realized that the night of the reunion. She had a confidence about her now that went with her professional demeanor. She'd also gotten curvier and had a quietly sexy way about her that stirred up buried physical needs. Was that only happening because it had been a long time since he'd wanted to have sex with a woman?

A voice in his head was yelling, *Not Mikala. She can't be an experiment to satisfy your libido.* Mikala had always been the kind of girl you respected...the kind of girl you waited for.

Where had *that* thought come from?

She finished with the pen and handed it to him so he could sign the log. Reaching for it, his fingers grazed hers. After he felt another jolt of attraction, he noticed such startled awareness in her eyes that he found it captivating. But he *couldn't* be captivated by Mikala. She was going to be working with his son. He couldn't—wouldn't—mess with that.

But when he studied her pretty face and her expressive dark brown eyes, he knew he faced a battle against attraction and chemistry and hormones he hadn't even known could roar through him anymore.

The last few years of his marriage to Kelly had become filled with tension. That tension translated into him burying himself in work…her already sleeping when he came home. Not much sex. Little intimacy. It had started with an argument they'd had when Luke was two. She'd revealed she'd stopped her birth control pills on purpose when they were dating because she'd wanted to get married! He'd been unwilling to let his own marriage disintegrate the way his parents' had and he'd held on to hope that he and Kelly could fix whatever was wrong. He'd been determined to make sure Luke's life wouldn't be marred by divorce the way his had.

But he'd never quite gotten over the pain of her lie.

Mikala didn't say much as she pointed out the fifth-grade classrooms and the arts center. A few kids waved at her as the bell rang and students headed for their buses. She stopped to introduce him to one of the teachers and then they made their way to a room at the end of the hall.

When they stepped inside, Dawson realized this was Mikala's domain. There was a keyboard, a box of tambourines, several large bright balls and several recorders on the top of a bookshelf. A chord chart hung on one wall and photographs of dancers on another.

"You're part-time but you have your own office?"

"Basically I'm an independent contractor. This room is in the older part of the building with thick walls, so it's perfect for music therapy. I coordinate my sessions with the guidance counselor and I also sub when the music teacher's sick."

"You're one busy lady—private clients, this and helping your aunt with the B and B."

"I like to keep busy. That keeps me out of trouble."

He had a feeling Mikala didn't get into trouble very often. He found himself way too curious about how she lived her life. "Have you ever *been* in trouble?"

"You mean besides the night of the prom?"

"Yes."

She looked over to her desk as if the subject made her uncomfortable, as if in some way his question had something to do with *them*. "I don't look for trouble, Dawson. I keep my life uncomplicated."

Had it always been that way? Because of what had happened on prom night? In high school they'd seemed to have an undeniable bond. But they'd both backed away from it...until the night he'd rescued her. Had she had lovers the past fifteen years? Many? All of that was too personal to ask. After all, they really didn't know each other *now*.

Then why did it feel as if they did?

Dropping the subject because he saw she wanted to, he remarked, "Luke's always gravitated toward music, though I don't know why."

"Music is a great way for kids to express themselves. It stimulates and relaxes—" She stopped and smiled. "Don't get me started. I like what I do."

"So why music therapy instead of teaching?"

Quiet for a few moments, Mikala seemed to hesitate. Dawson guessed she didn't reveal her innermost thoughts and motives to many people. She hadn't changed completely from the quiet, deep-thinking girl she'd been.

Finally she explained, "I'd planned to teach. But then one of my professors in college—she was a violinist—had a friend who was in an accident and fell into a coma. Dorothy visited every day. She played her violin for her. But then she got to thinking about important events in her friend's life. She found the music that had been played at Cheryl's wedding and played the song Cheryl and her husband had danced to. And Cheryl woke up! Dorothy had been so excited that she told me about it. Was it coincidence she woke up during that song? No one will ever know. But the hope that idea carried was amazing. I think I decided that day I wanted to do more than just *teach* music."

Dawson witnessed the glistening emotion in Mikala's eyes that the story brought up in her.

It was only there a short time, though, as she crossed to her desk and fiddled with the corner of a paper on her blotter. "I seem to remember you played the guitar. Do you still?"

That guitar had been packed away for a long time. "I haven't picked it up in years."

"Why not?"

"No time."

At that she crinkled her nose.

Moving close enough to touch her, he asked, "What was that for?"

"We make time for what we want to make time for."

He didn't agree with that. "Sometimes there are demands on our time and we can't do what we want."

"I don't know, Dawson. We all prioritize. You said you were working long hours and didn't spend much time with Luke, but when you did, you enjoyed it. So what *kept* you from spending more time with him? I mean, why didn't you make him a priority?"

He couldn't tell if Mikala specifically meant to or not, but she was getting under his skin. He didn't like it. He didn't like the years-old attraction he was experiencing toward her *or* the way she was probing. Instinctively he knew she wouldn't accept "work" as an answer, so he really thought about what she'd asked.

He gave an honest answer that caused his gut to burn. "I didn't like the strain between me and Kelly that last year before she died." He shook his head. "When I came into the house, she left." That was hard to admit to anyone, especially Mikala. But he'd already realized she wouldn't accept anything less than complete honesty.

To his relief she didn't ask more questions about his marriage. "Did you do things together as a family?"

Dawson didn't know if Mikala the therapist was asking, or Mikala the friend. He gave a shrug. "Not usually. I drove Luke to his Little League games. Kelly took him to his music lessons. I played catch with him in the backyard. She took him on play dates."

"That happens with a lot of parents," Mikala said, seeming to understand.

He didn't feel any judgment from her and that made him feel less defensive. "I wish I knew how to get Luke looking forward to moving here."

"Does he like animals? Has he ever asked for a pet, a dog, maybe?"

He took another step closer to Mikala. "You really do know kids."

She laughed, a sound that resonated with him, that made his heart ache a little. Because he hadn't known much laughter in the past two years.

"I'm good at what I do, Dawson. Besides, I get around. I often babysit for Clay and Celeste's little girl, Abby."

"Clay has emailed me photos and video clips. She's a charmer."

"Yes, she is."

He noticed a wistfulness in Mikala's voice. Did she want children of her own? Did she feel a biological clock ticking? Why hadn't she married before now?

Veering away from that train of thought, he said, "I'm considering getting Luke a dog. It's a good idea after we settle in. Luke's old enough now to be responsible."

"Did *you* have pets?" she asked with a smile.

Dawson wished he'd had a pet. Maybe his house wouldn't have seemed so cold. "No, no pets. Dad was always at the mill. Mom involved herself in clubs and charity work. She raised money for a lot of causes."

"As an only child, you must have had their full attention."

He gave an offhanded laugh. "Yep, full attention." He wasn't going to say more. After all, Mikala didn't have to know everything about him in order to help his son. No need at all. She didn't need to know that his parents' marriage had been cold, that they'd seemed to live separate lives, that they had seemed to stay together for convenience sake, for his sake or maybe for the sake of their finances.

This room seemed to magnify everything they were saying to each other, making it important. He turned the tables on her. "Didn't your aunt dote on *you?*"

A guarded look came into Mikala's eyes, and he recognized it as one she'd used even as a teenager.

"She did." Mikala said simply.

"And your mom became a famous fashion designer who just visited on weekends?"

"Not that often," Mikala offered nonchalantly. "When she had time."

"When did she leave Miners Bluff?"

"Dawson, it doesn't matter."

"I've been answering *your* questions," he reminded her.

"That's different! I mean, I need to know background information in order to help Luke."

"All of your questions had to do with background information?" He didn't know why he was pushing this, but he was.

He saw the flush steal over her face, and he knew he'd hit the mark. She was interested in his life, just as he was interested in hers.

"Maybe not all," she admitted. "After all, we're sort of catching up."

Yes, they were. "There's a motto my parents lived by—*appearances count.* We all lived by it."

"I'm not sure what you mean."

What did it matter if he told her now? "What was

private stayed private. We pretended everything was all right, even when it wasn't. I have a feeling you might have done a lot of that, too."

She didn't say whether he was right or whether he was wrong. But there was something in the way the corner of her mouth quivered a little, in the way she nervously pushed her hair behind her ear that told him he'd hit a sore point for her, too. Mikala pretended her mother's desertion didn't matter. Maybe that's why she'd kept a certain distance from everyone. Maybe that's why her friendliness and maybe even her compassion were defenses. She got close to her friends, but didn't let her friends get *too* close to *her*.

Except there hadn't been any distance between them the night of prom, and there hadn't been distance between them for the few minutes they'd danced the night of the reunion. Now he wasn't sure what was happening with her. Maybe they *were* just catching up, but the connection he felt to her unnerved him.

Cutting off whatever was going on, he said, "I'd better get to the office or I'll be late for my appointment."

At first he thought Mikala looked hurt he'd broken off the conversation so abruptly. But then that flicker of emotion was gone and she looked so…neutral…he wondered if he'd glimpsed it at all.

"You go on," she said amiably. "I brought my flash drive with some files I need to load on the computer. I'll be waiting in the office for you when you finish. Philip doesn't waste time. He'll probably have you in and out of there in fifteen minutes unless you have a lot of questions."

"I've already spoken with him on the phone. You're

right. He's crisp, but thorough. I'll see you in a little while."

He left Mikala in the music room, thinking about his connection with her that seemed to defy time.

Forty-five minutes later, Mikala wondered how to make the awkwardness between her and Dawson dissipate. They'd driven back to the B and B in his luxury SUV, listening to music he'd programmed in. She wondered about the life he'd led in Phoenix. From his supple leather jacket to his low Italian boots, she could tell he was used to the finer things in life.

As they stood in the kitchen, their history and unspoken bond vibrating between them, Mikala gestured at the counter. "Help yourself to anything you want in the refrigerator or the cookie jar. This will be your home for a while."

"Not until I come back. I feel like I'm taking advantage of your aunt by staying in that suite tonight. I could just sleep on the sofa—then she wouldn't have to change the bed."

"We might not even register any guests between now and the fifteenth. Don't worry about it, Dawson. Be comfortable tonight."

They were talking about beds and that wasn't any more comfortable than anything else.

There was a sudden knock on the kitchen door. Dawson asked, "Expecting someone?"

"No, but I do have a session in about an hour. Maybe my client had the time wrong." But when she opened the door, she smiled widely.

Celeste Sullivan stood there with her almost-four-year-old daughter, Abby, holding her hand. Abby immediately held her arms up to Mikala for a hug.

"Hi, honey. What an unexpected surprise!"

Celeste laughed. "Abby was restless and Clay won't be back until late tonight, so we thought we'd come for a visit. If it's a bad time, we'll go downtown to the library instead."

"No! Come on in. Wait until you see who's here."

When Celeste came in, she spotted Dawson and immediately crossed to him to give him a hug. "It's good to see you again! Clay said you might be moving back here. Is that official?"

"It will be in a couple of weeks. I just came up to find a place to stay and to register Luke at school."

"Where are you going to be staying?"

"Right here. Aunt Anna says I'll be doing her a favor using one of her suites, so Luke and I will be on the third floor."

Abby came over to stand beside her mother and looked up at Dawson.

He crouched down to her level. "Hi, there. Your daddy has emailed me pictures of you and you look even prettier in person."

Mikala's heart warmed at Dawson's tone. He obviously knew how to talk to kids.

"I'm Dawson," he said, extending his hand out to her.

She ceremoniously shook it. "I'm Abby."

"It's official. We've met." He rose to his feet. "And now I have to give my dad a call and check on my son," he said to Celeste and Mikala. "If there are any problems, I'll have to drive back tonight."

It was quite evident that Dawson was putting Luke

first, and Mikala admired him for doing that. Sometimes it was really difficult for a parent to put aside his own concerns for his child's.

Dawson said to Celeste, "I hope I'll be seeing you after we get settled in. It will be nice to talk to Clay face-to-face instead of on the phone."

"I'm sure he's looking forward to that, too. And Zack. He and Jenny are on their honeymoon now but should be back by the time you move here."

"Sounds good," Dawson agreed, his gaze meeting Mikala's. She knew what he was thinking. He wouldn't be socializing much with old friends like Clay Sullivan and Zack Decker if his problems with Luke didn't settle down.

Once Dawson had left the kitchen, Abby ran over to the cookie jar and looked up at it. "Can I have one, Mommy?"

"Sure, if you have a glass of milk to go with it."

Abby was amenable to that, so Mikala took milk from the refrigerator and poured her a glass, made tea for herself and Celeste.

When they were all seated at the table enjoying their snacks, Celeste asked Mikala, "What was that look you gave Dawson before he left to go upstairs?"

"What look?"

"I'm not sure. Like the two of you have a secret. I know he's moving back here so you can treat Luke. Clay told me."

"You know I can't talk about that."

"I know." Celeste waited a couple of beats, then nonchalantly prompted, "There were rumors back in high school about the two of you."

"What kind of rumors?" Mikala was absolutely

surprised. She'd never given anyone reason to start a rumor about her and Dawson.

"There was talk that Dawson was going to ask you to the prom."

"Why didn't *I* ever hear about it?"

"Because what's-his-name asked you."

"What's-his-name only asked me because all the popular girls were taken."

"Mikala! You never did have a true image of yourself back then. You were pretty but quiet, sometimes even more than I was."

Celeste had always been the opposite of her twin sister, Zoie, who had been an extreme extrovert. That's why Zoie had initially caught Clay's eye, even marrying him after high school. Clay hadn't realized until after his divorce from Zoie that Celeste and he were much more suited for each other—especially since Celeste had been Abby's surrogate mother. After the reunion last summer their bond and chemistry had transformed into love, and they became a family.

Celeste *had* been quiet in high school, but in a different way than Mikala. Mikala had stood her ground when she'd had to. She'd always championed the underdog. If she'd kept to herself for the most part, that was because she'd felt so different from her other classmates who had moms and dads, a different kind of family than she did. Only with her small circle of friends had she felt more secure.

Even back then, she'd kept her own counsel and was truly surprised about the rumor. "I had hoped Dawson would ask me to the prom. But when Carson asked me first, I accepted because I wanted to go so badly. I wanted to feel pretty and grown-up, like the

popular girls. Dawson and I were friends and I didn't
think he thought of me that way—as a date. At least I
didn't think that until—" Uh-oh. She shouldn't have
let that slip.

"Until what?"

"Until the night of the prom."

Mikala still remembered vividly exactly what had
happened. The night had started off with her feeling
almost glamorous in a pink chiffon dress with her
aunt's aurora borealis crystals around her neck and
on her ears. She'd worn white silk high-heeled sandals
and carried a beaded bag. Carson had picked her up
and brought her a beautiful corsage. They'd struggled
making small talk, but that had been okay. After all,
they hadn't known each other very well. After they'd
arrived at the prom and danced a couple of dances,
Carson had gone outside with his buddies for a while.
Dawson, who'd been there by himself because his date
had caught the flu, had asked her to dance.

With him standing before her, looking so handsome
and grown-up, his gaze making her head swim, she'd
thought about whether she should or shouldn't dance
with him. Even though she'd wanted to more than anything, she'd come with Carson. Yet other couples were
mixing it up, exchanging partners, and there hadn't
seemed to be any harm in just one dance.

But the moment Dawson had taken her hand in his
and wrapped his arm around her, she'd known this
was a dance she was going to remember *forever*. Their
gazes had met as he'd looked down at her, and they'd
both smiled. He hadn't said anything, just held her a
little closer. She'd nestled into him as if she'd belonged

there. In some ways the dance had seemed like a lifetime. In others it had only been a second long.

When Carson had returned to the cafeteria, she'd seen him the same time as Dawson. Their song ended and Dawson had given her hand a slight squeeze as he'd let go, almost as if he didn't *want* to let go. Then she'd joined Carson at their table, smelling liquor on his breath. Despite her growing misgivings, she'd gone with him to his car. Wanting to feel accepted again?

What a stupid thing to do.

The flow of memory breaking, she looked at Celeste. "You know what happened with Carson that night." Mikala glanced at Abby. She wasn't going to say anything that little ears shouldn't hear.

"You told me and Jenny the next day. You told us how Dawson rescued you and took you home."

"And then he disappeared. I didn't see or hear from him again until last summer at the reunion." She and Jenny and Celeste had never talked about Dawson and what had happened. That had been in the past. Though the melody of the song they'd danced to had played in her head over the years, each time bringing back the vivid sensation of Dawson's arms around her as they danced.

"All I heard was that his grandfather fell and his mom took Dawson with her to Wisconsin to take care of her father. Dawson's grades were good enough without finals and the school mailed him his diploma. But he and his mom never came back," Mikala mused.

"No, and his dad moved to Phoenix."

"I wonder if that's when his parents' marriage broke up?"

"I guess," Celeste responded. "Clay says Dawson

never talks about that time. But eventually he moved to Phoenix with his dad, earned a business degree and became CEO of the company his dad had started."

"Interesting," Mikala mused.

"His life or him?" Celeste asked, with a twinkle in her eye.

Mikala thought about Dawson's life and what he and Luke were going through. "Dawson's still recovering from his wife's death. And me? Well, you know trust is an issue for me."

"It isn't just *trust,* Mikala. You don't think you're sexy enough for a man to want you."

Mikala nodded to Abby, but Abby was dipping her biscotti into her milk glass, slurping it up and then chewing on the cookie.

Finally Mikala admitted, "My last relationship proved it."

"That was a long time ago."

"I haven't forgotten it."

"That's the problem. Maybe Dawson can help you forget about it."

"Don't go there," Mikala warned.

Celeste just shrugged and sipped her tea.

That evening Mikala stood at the door to Dawson's suite, not knowing whether she should be angry at her aunt or just amused by her. Mikala had had an early evening session and had come in to find her aunt putting together a dinner platter. She'd made sloppy joes, oven-baked potatoes and some kind of broccoli casserole with cheese. She'd handed the platter to Mikala and said, "Why don't you take this up to Dawson? He'll probably be glad not to have to go out again."

"Aunt Anna—" Mikala wanted to start a conversation about why her aunt was doing this.

But always intuitive where her niece was concerned, her aunt had just patted her on the shoulder and said, "It's just a friendly gesture, Mikala. Go on before it gets cold."

Her aunt had done so much for her, Mikala couldn't refuse her anything.

From the hall she spotted light under Dawson's door and knocked lightly. But Dawson didn't answer.

Go away, or not go away? The food on the plate was warm but wouldn't stay that way long.

Since the door was slightly ajar— She wasn't going to go inside unless he was right *there.*

Pushing the door open a little more, she saw Dawson *was* right there, stretched out on the sofa on his side, fast asleep. He was too tall for the couch. His head looked as if it was in an uncomfortable position on the sofa's arm and he'd hunched a throw pillow under his shoulder. With his shoes off, he barely fit. She remembered what she'd thought when she'd first seen him at the reunion. He was a multimillionaire, the CEO of his own company, confident, charismatic, sexy. Now as she studied him, she saw a bit of the vulnerability he wanted no one to see, a hint of the boy she'd once known.

As if he could hear her thoughts, he opened his eyes and spotted her.

She felt as if she'd been doing something wrong. "Your door was open," she said quickly. "Aunt Anna thought you'd like dinner. It's hot, so I didn't want to just take it back to the kitchen. I thought maybe you were watching TV and didn't hear my knock."

He levered himself up, ran his hand through his hair and motioned to the laptop on the coffee table. "I took some calls and worked for a while. Then I thought I'd just close my eyes for a couple of minutes before I got back to it."

Crossing to the sofa, she sat down beside him, setting the food on the coffee table. She imagined he'd had lots of sleepless nights in the past few weeks, lots of days filled with worry and stress about Luke along with what he was going to do about his business, his work, and a new life in Miners Bluff.

"Maybe some food will get the juices flowing again."

As soon as those words came out of her mouth, she knew she should have watched what she said more carefully. His eyes went deeper green with a simmering intensity she'd seen there before.

Yet he didn't comment, just eyed the platter appreciatively. "Your aunt knows the way to a man's heart. Her kindness is limitless." He paused, thought about what he was going to say, and then obviously decided to say it. "I see that same kindness in you."

For the second time in one day, she felt heat come to her cheeks. She *never* blushed. "Thank you. Go ahead and eat before it gets cold." She would have risen to her feet, but he held her arm and she stayed where she was.

"Thank you."

"I haven't done anything yet."

"You're helping to make this transition easier. I called Dad when I came up here."

"And?" she prompted.

"And...Luke is giving him all the reasons why

he should stay with him instead of moving up here with me."

"Oh, Dawson, that has to be so hard to hear."

"I wouldn't know. Luke won't talk to me. What happens if he gets here and barricades himself in his room like he does at home?"

"I really don't think that will happen. At least, not all of the time. We'll have surprise on our side."

"Surprise?"

She counted on children's curiosity a lot of the time whether it was to try something new or just to coax them to talk. "He doesn't know Anna and he doesn't know me. Even the weather's different here. Who can resist looking up to Moonshadow Mountain and Feather Peak? There will be plenty of things to interest him, and lots of people who can get through to him. His natural curiosity will help, too. I know things seem bad right now, but try to stay optimistic. Try to see all the things that will connect you to Luke rather than tear him away."

Dawson was looking at her differently than he ever had before. She'd caught a glimpse of desire the night of the prom *and* the night of the reunion. But now, there was something behind that desire. Emotion? Feeling for her and a past they'd shared? That's what caught her in its trap. That's what took her by surprise. That's what helped good sense flee and made "the moment" become all-important. As an adult the moment had never been all-important for her. She always analyzed the consequences. But Dawson kickstarted a passion she didn't even know she possessed, without even a touch or a word or a kiss.

Suddenly he was murmuring, "Mikala, you've always been special to me. I always wondered what might have happened if I hadn't left Miners Bluff."

"What do you think would have happened?" she whispered, knowing this moment was important, not wanting to shatter it.

His hand went to the nape of her neck. "I think we would have dated. We might have gotten close." He tipped her lips up to his. "And maybe..."

As Dawson's mouth took possession of hers, she wrapped her arms around his neck and fell into the scent and feel of him. The kiss started slowly, like a wonderful melody that kept on playing. Then it changed verses as it increased in intensity, meandering into the refrain and began all over again. She'd always wondered what kissing Dawson would feel like. It was a symphony she never wanted to stop, a haunting ballad that reached down into her heart, making her feel emotions she'd never let surface.

Sudden need rose in her, sending fire into every part of her body. She didn't even know the woman who was responding to the touch of his tongue...to the angle of his lips...to the deepening of their passion that left her totally without breath. She ran her hand through his thick, tawny hair. As his hands stroked up and down her back, she trembled.

Suddenly everything stopped—the new melody, the riot of sensations, the rippling adventure of wanting and being wanted in return.

He pulled away with a ragged oath and started shaking his head. "I never expected—" He stopped.

She didn't give him a chance to say more. Somehow she managed to pull herself together, put distance between them and pretend she was perfectly all right.

"Enjoy your dinner," she murmured as she fled to the door.

He called out to her, but she ignored him as she ran down the stairs, putting the moment behind her once and for all.

She hoped.

Chapter Three

Almost two weeks later Mikala watched Dawson and Luke carry their belongings into the Purple Pansy. Luke looked like his dad—same color hair and eyes, same jaw that would become more defined like Dawson's as he got older.

She could already sense the tension between father and son. It was obvious that communication was almost null and void between them.

Since Dawson had left, she'd tried to forget about the kiss, and their awkward goodbye the next morning. Now, as she watched Luke and Dawson interact—or rather *not* interact—she knew she had her work cut out for her on all fronts, both personal as well as professional.

Aunt Anna stood at the counter, adding peas to the slow cooker as Dawson and Luke entered the kitchen once more, ready to return to the SUV for another load.

She introduced herself to Luke and asked, "What do you think of vegetable soup for supper?"

His gaze glanced from hers to Mikala's to his dad's. Finally he shrugged.

But Anna was having none of that. "You've got to tell me what you like and don't like. If you don't like vegetable soup, say so."

The ten-year-old pushed his blond-brown hair from his forehead, then shrugged again. "It's okay, I guess. I like burgers better."

"Of course you do," Anna agreed with a smile. "But burgers every night aren't healthy. I'll make you one, though, if you promise to have some soup, too."

Dawson interrupted. "You don't have to make anything special. You don't have to make anything at all. We can go out to eat."

"Nonsense!" Anna swished her hand dismissively. Then she took the cookie jar from the counter and opened the lid, holding it out to Luke. "Homemade biscotti. There's chocolate milk in the refrigerator if you're interested."

Mikala went over to a cupboard, opened it and removed a glass. "Just so you know, the glasses are in this cupboard. While you're here, you're welcome to make yourself at home."

He took the glass Mikala offered, said "Thanks" and went to the refrigerator. He easily found the chocolate milk and poured himself some.

Dawson hovered, and to get him to stop, Mikala suggested, "I'll help you bring in the rest of your things."

"I can get it," he began, but then caught her glance and understood. "Right."

They were no sooner out the door when he blew out a breath. "I knew this wasn't going to be easy, but still...he wouldn't talk to me the whole drive here."

"Each day isn't going to be the end of something, Dawson. Like you said, hopefully moving here will be the beginning. Try to remember that."

He stopped. "Are you preaching the value of optimism? Because I've tried to be optimistic over the past year. It hasn't worked out very well."

"I'm sorry. I didn't mean it that way."

His defensiveness dissipated. "Sorry. Being cooped up in a car for three hours with a sulking ten-year-old kind of frayed my edges."

"Aunt Anna will work her magic. Come on, let's see what else you have to bring in."

At the SUV, Mikala went around to the back and reached for a very expensive suitcase. She could tell by the designer logo.

"Hold on." Dawson took it from her before she could lift it to the ground. "That's pretty heavy. I'll get it."

She flexed her arm. "I guess you haven't seen my muscles," she joked.

Finally he broke into a smile. His fingers surrounded her upper arm and he squeezed gently. It was supposed to be a playful touch. She knew that. But it wasn't so playful as she looked up into his eyes.

He removed his fingers and kidded, "Yep, there are muscles there. But I'll still carry the suitcase."

"Chivalry must be alive and well." She grabbed a duffel bag and a basketball. "I guess a backboard's in Luke's future."

"Maybe just mine. Anything I'm interested in, doesn't interest him."

"Have you asked him why?"

"Does it snow on Feather Peak?" After she arched a brow at him, he ran his hand through his hair.

"If I seem defensive, it's because I am. That kiss when I was here last—" He stopped, obviously frustrated with himself because it had happened. "I see our move here and Luke's therapy as a real chance to put everything right. I want to give him a more ordinary life without full security house alarms, gated communities, private schools. I guess I'm trying to leave 'rich' behind. I don't want to throw a new life off track. I feel like I've failed him up till now. I wasn't the greatest dad. Now he's lost his mom and I'll never be able to make up for that."

"You're right." She couldn't tell Dawson he wasn't. But she also couldn't let him take on a responsibility that could be too heavy for anyone. "You don't have to make up for Kelly dying, and you can't. You just need to be there for Luke."

Dawson mulled that over as he picked up the suitcase as if it weighed nothing at all and they began walking toward the bed-and-breakfast again. When they reached the porch, he asked, "When will you start therapy with him?"

"Actually I want *you* to start therapy with him."

He set the suitcase on the porch floor. "What do you mean?"

"If you and Luke go up to your suite, what's going to happen?"

"He'll probably go into his bedroom and shut the door."

"Exactly. So instead, surprise him. Why don't you take him into town and show him around? Point out

where you lived, where you went to school and anything else that's meaningful to you and could be meaningful to him. After you return, I'll talk to him. Not a
formal therapy session, but a get-to-know-you session.
Maybe it will help him feel more confident about at-
tending a new school, which is a big adjustment. We
can both help him ease into it."

Dawson stared up at the winter blue sky, at the pine
forests that fringed so much of Miners Bluff. "And if
he doesn't say a word to me in the SUV?"

"He doesn't have to. Just talk to him. Let the memories come…and whatever emotions come with them."

"Coming back here and remembering could be painful. The idea of it makes me feel…vulnerable. I haven't
been vulnerable to anyone in a very long time."

She could empathize. True intimacy demanded vulnerability and she was afraid of letting her guard down
as much as anyone. "Nothing's going to happen overnight, or in one ride around town. But if you can just
share one memory with him from childhood—something that affected your life in some way—and he hears
the truth in that, he might look at you differently." Her
tone took on a lighter note. "He might actually see that
you're not just his dad, you're a *person*."

"If you want Luke to see me as a person, we really
have a lot of work to do."

She laughed.

Dawson looked as if he wanted to give her a hug…or
something. Instead he lifted the suitcase again, opened
the door and headed into the kitchen where the biscotti
jar and chocolate milk had brought back memories of
their teenage years around that kitchen table. Maybe
Dawson and Luke weren't the only ones who would

have to let a few walls down. Mikala's biggest problem would be separating the personal from the professional.

But she could and would do that. She really had no choice. And while she was doing it, she would *not* think about Dawson's kiss.

An hour later Dawson and Luke both stood in Mikala's studio looking uncomfortable. If that was any indication of how their drive had gone...

"Luke, why don't you go into the music room and make yourself at home. I just have to talk to your dad for a few minutes and then I'll be in."

Luke gave them both an I-don't-want-to-do-this look, but wandered into the music room and went over to the bench at the piano. Mikala wasn't surprised. That's where he probably felt the most comfortable.

She said to Dawson, "Let's step outside a minute. I don't want to leave him too long."

They were hardly on the stoop of the studio when Dawson said with some disappointment, "He didn't say a word. I was hoping... We drove downtown around the park and I tried to explain the celebrations held there. You know. The happy times I remembered. Then I took him past our old house—*my* old house."

She knew Dawson needed some of this return-to-the-past as much as Luke did, so she asked, "How did it look?"

"Different, yet the same. New shutters, beige trim instead of white, brown roof instead of red. But the yard... I remembered practicing my pitching in that yard. Tossing baskets at the backboard on the garage. Then the garage reminded me of the weeks I worked on my first car in there. I tried to share all that with Luke, but he just sat there as if nothing I said mattered."

"He heard you, Dawson."

"How can you be so sure?"

"I'm sure because I can tell from Luke's comments and his facial expressions and his body language that he hears what everybody's saying. He's in culture shock right now. You've moved him from the only home he knows. Give him time to settle in. Give yourself time, too."

"What do you plan to accomplish today?"

"Not a whole lot. I just want Luke to get used to me. We'll get into all the rest of it soon enough."

"If you run over, I pay overtime."

"We'll talk about it if it happens."

"Mikala, I *am* paying you for this. I won't do it any other way."

Gazing into Dawson's eyes, she saw the integrity he'd always possessed, fairness that always made him a good leader. But it wasn't integrity or fairness that practically mesmerized her as she stared into his eyes. It was something so much deeper than either of them were going to act on.

Yet even as she thought it, she noticed the tiny scar along his jaw that he hadn't had as a teenager. She also caught a glimpse of a few silver strands in the hair at his temples. There was a swirl of chest hair in the V-neck of his shirt. In high school she'd seen him at their favorite swimming hole in his bathing suit and thought no boy in their class had looked as good.

Pushing all those memories aside, she said, "I've got to go in to Luke. Just trust me, Dawson."

"I'll try. I'll be up in my suite. Call my cell if you

need me. In fact, call my cell when you're finished and I'll come back over for him."

Dawson was hovering again and he had to break the habit. "He's my last appointment today. It might be better if we just walk over to the bed-and-breakfast and he comes and finds you."

"Right. I guess I'm supposed to give him space."

As she turned toward the studio, Dawson caught her hand. His fingers folded around hers, and she thought, *No, don't touch me. I feel too much when you do.*

"I'll talk to you later," he said as if he expected results from her meeting with Luke.

She didn't go over the ground rules again. She'd already told him she wouldn't be able to report what Luke said without his permission. Yet she nodded, slipped her hand from Dawson's and went inside.

When she returned to the studio, Luke didn't pay her any mind. She went to her desk and picked up her legal pad, then crossed to the doorway of the music room. "Where would you like to sit and talk? In here? Or in my office?"

Luke sat at the piano with his fingers on the keys, yet he wasn't playing.

"I don't want to sit either place."

"I know you don't."

He brought his hands down on the piano into two loud chords. Mikala quietly sat in the chair beside the piano bench and waited.

After a while Luke asked, "Aren't you going to say something?"

"I know you've seen counselors before."

"A psychiatrist and a psychologist. What are you?"

"Didn't your dad tell you?"

"He just said you're an old friend he went to school with, and you're a music therapist. But I don't know what that's got to do with anything."

"Your dad told me you can memorize pieces on the piano without a lot of trouble. That's pretty cool."

"I play them and I remember them."

"Would you play something for me?" She was fully prepared for him to say no.

"All right," he agreed, and she thought maybe he was going to cooperate. But then he played random notes, discordant sequences, a melody with only a hint of a pattern. When he was finished, he looked at her as if he expected her to scold him.

"How did you feel while you were playing?"

His mouth opened in surprise as if he hadn't expected the question. He clammed up, took his hands from the keyboard and just settled them on his jeans.

"This isn't about what you play or you don't play," she said, responding to his silence. "We'll have another session later in the week, after you get accustomed to school here. I'd like to know what kind of music you like. So it would be terrific if you make me a list—singers, styles, individual pieces. Do you have any sheet music?"

"Some," he muttered warily.

"Good. I'd like to take a look at it."

"What if I don't want to play the piano?"

"Would you like to learn something else?" She gestured toward the violin, the guitar, the oboe.

"Maybe I don't want to *play* anything. Maybe I don't want to *talk* about anything."

"Well, then I guess it will be really quiet in here. We're going to spend some time together, Luke. We'll do whatever works. You can tell me what you're thinking and what you're feeling. If you don't want to tell me with words, you can tell me with music or even a tambourine. If all else fails, I'll bring in a set of drums and you can beat away some of that pent-up anger you've got inside of you."

"How do you know I'm mad?" He sounded surprised at her perception.

"I can hear it in some of the things you say, and I know you've been getting into fights at school."

"Those people I saw before—Miss Bracken, Dr. Johnston. They said they'd make the anger go away. But they didn't." He stared down at his sneakers rather than up at her and mumbled, "I don't even know why I'm mad."

"Usually when someone feels mad, they feel sad or hurt first. Then they don't know what to do with that and they get angry. That might be something you can think about till our next session."

His eyes finally met hers, eyes that were so much like Dawson's. "I didn't want to come here. I don't want to *be* here."

"I can understand that you don't want to be here. But you are, and I'd like to help you make everything a little better."

"By using music?"

"Exactly."

He looked curious about the method. If curiosity was all she could get from him for today, she'd take it.

When Mikala walked Luke into the kitchen, conversation there stopped. Dawson had obviously been talking to Anna, but the silence wasn't a welcome introduction to supper.

"Everything smells great." Mikala knew the best tactic was to try to get everything back on an easy footing again. The soup was still simmering in the crock pot and corn bread sat on the counter. All of the aromas permeated the kitchen while Mikala could hear burgers sizzling under the broiler.

"Are you hungry?" Anna asked Luke.

Again that shrug that could be as frustrating as silence.

Anna smiled anyway. "There's a powder room down the hall. Why don't you go there and wash up. Ketchup or mustard for your burger?"

"Both," Luke tossed over his shoulder as he left the kitchen.

Once the kitchen door had swung closed, Dawson looked at Mikala expectantly.

She went to the sink where he was standing and kept her voice very low. "Expectation is all over your face. You can't look at Luke like that when he comes back from a session."

"I can't ask what happened?"

"Wouldn't you rather he tell you on his own?"

"I doubt if *that's* going to happen."

"Wait until it does."

"Give me a hint?"

Although Mikala was used to dealing with worried parents, she found discussing this with Dawson even harder. "You really have to give Luke time."

"I don't want the situation to get worse," he admitted.

"Give your life in Miners Bluff a chance to work."

When Dawson frowned, she knew he was impatient. He just wanted his life and Luke's to be settled again. She couldn't promise him it would get settled anytime soon.

With the pause in their conversation, Anna said casually, "I was telling Dawson about the ice skating rink, The McDougall Center. I told him you enjoy skating there and thought they might, too. Great Sunday afternoon activity."

"I thought we could check it out tomorrow," Dawson said. After Luke returned to the kitchen, conversation at supper started slowly. Luke ate his burger while Anna made small talk about Miners Bluff. After the burger he took a look at the soup, ate a spoonful and then another. Soon his spoon tapped the bottom of his bowl.

He looked up at Mikala. "Do you see people at night?"

Mikala had no idea where this was going. "Sometimes I have an evening session, but not every night. What were you thinking about?"

"The piano."

She caught on immediately. "Would you like to use it?"

Luke gave a little shrug.

A shrug could mean so many things, but right now she knew it meant he'd like to, but didn't know if he should ask.

"I usually keep the studio locked unless I'm there. But if it's free, you can go in and play as long as you'd like."

"Cool," he said with a nod.

Dawson looked at his son and then at Mikala.

"There's an ice skating rink near Moonshadow Mountain." He asked Luke, "What would you think about trying it out tomorrow afternoon?"

"I haven't been ice skating very much."

"Phoenix has an indoor rink. We've gone there a few times," Dawson explained. Then he turned back to his son. "Ice skating's like riding a bike. You don't forget how. You've got great balance. I can tell when we play basketball. I thought it would give both of us a way to work off some energy until we can get a place with a hoop."

Luke seemed to think about it, and then his gaze targeted Mikala. "Do you ice skate?"

"As often as I can when the rink's open."

"Do they have a game room?" Dawson's son asked.

She had to smile. "Yes, they do. And a snack bar. They've got great hot dogs with everything on them."

"You could come along," Luke offered, offhandedly as if it didn't matter. Maybe he wanted her to act as a buffer.

She didn't want to crowd this father and son who really needed to talk to each other. "I'll be going to church in the morning with Aunt Anna, and then visiting with a friend afterward. But I can meet you there."

"How about if we meet there around three?" Dawson suggested.

Mikala looked directly at Luke. "Would that be okay with you?"

Luke pushed his soup bowl aside, nodded, then asked, "Can I be excused? I want to call Granddad."

Dawson took his cell phone from his pocket and handed it to him. "Go ahead. I'll be up soon."

Luke took the phone and exited the kitchen.

"I have to be going, too." Anna pushed her chair away from the table. "Silas is picking me up. He's taking me to one of those old movies downtown."

Pleased Zack Decker's father, Silas, and her aunt were "dating" regularly, Mikala told Anna, "I'll clean up. You go get ready."

Before Anna left the kitchen, she turned to Dawson. "It will be nice having you and your son around." Then she smiled and left Mikala alone with him.

Feeling fidgety, Mikala decided cleaning up was easier than sitting there staring into Dawson's green eyes. "If you'd like dessert, I'll wrap up two pieces of pie and you can take them up to your suite."

She went to the pie holder to escape being too close.

But Dawson followed her and put his hand on her shoulder. She went stone still. The heat of his touch radiated through her sweater down into her bones. Her awareness of him must have shown in her eyes when she turned to face him because he quickly dropped his hand to his side.

"Are you sure you want to go tomorrow?" he asked. "Luke put you on the spot."

"I like to skate. If I start getting in your way, I'll make a quick exit."

Dawson's features relaxed a bit as he smiled. "I think he likes you."

"Not necessarily. He's in a strange place with people he doesn't know," she pointed out. "I was straight up with him about what we're going to do in our sessions, so maybe he sees me as a port in the storm right now. But when I start probing and he begins to feel uncomfortable, he might not like me so much."

"Who are you visiting with tomorrow?"

The question was so off-topic she was speechless.

Dawson smiled again and gave a shrug that reminded her of Luke's. "You can tell me it's none of my business. I'm just curious. Is it a date?"

Just how much did she want Dawson to be involved in her life? She was going to become involved in his, that was for sure. But this didn't have to be a two-way street.

Seeing her obvious hesitancy, he said, "Never mind." Turning away from her, he pulled two dishes from the cupboard, ready to cut his own pie.

Impulsively she caught his arm.

He stopped moving, and she stilled. When they gazed into each other's eyes, time suddenly stopped. She wasn't sure what she saw on Dawson's face—longing, desire, something else. She felt her heart ticking fast, heat infusing her cheeks.

Releasing her hold, she took a deep breath. "No date tomorrow. I'm meeting Jenny. She and Zack are back from their honeymoon. He's videoconferencing about his new project tomorrow afternoon, so she and I are going to catch up."

A few beats of the kitchen clock ticked off the silence before Dawson asked, "Are you dating anyone?"

"No, I'm not."

"Why?"

"I have a busy life."

He cocked his head and studied her. "There are a lot of single guys in this town, some from our class—Noah Stone, Riley O'Rourke, Brody Hazlett, for starters."

"Noah and I are friends. As chief of police, he's also

involved in several after-school programs for children, so sometimes we work together."

"And Riley?"

"Riley has partnered up with Clay in his wilderness guiding business. He's a busy guy."

"Then there's Brody."

"I think Brody was interested in Jenny, but when Zack came back, that put a damper on all *his* plans."

"I'm sure there are other men in town who would like to ask you out. Why don't you go?"

Having analyzed her own life many times, Mikala understood she hadn't felt wanted as a child. With a father who left before she was born and a mother who hadn't wanted a child at all, she'd always been racked by the insecurity that she wasn't good enough—or pretty enough. Then when Alan had dumped her, it had reinforced it all. She looked down at her sneakers and felt all those old insecurities rising up again. "I just don't date much, Dawson. Let's just leave it at that."

"But why? Mikala, you're one of the most attractive, put-together, intelligent women I know."

When she looked up at him, she couldn't keep the sadness from her voice. "Look, you really don't know me anymore. I don't do one-night stands. I don't go out just for the— Don't you get it, Dawson? I'm just not like that. Can we please drop this?"

She wasn't going to confide in him about the failure of her one serious relationship—not when she was attracted to him, not when she was going to treat his son, not when they'd both be sleeping under the same roof. He looked as if he wanted to kiss her again. The problem was, she wanted him to. But that was *not* going to happen.

Slipping away from his hands and from him, she murmured, "I'll get that pie ready for you."

In a way she wished they could stay strangers. Then she wouldn't feel so vulnerable...then she wouldn't feel as if letting him into her life again would only cause her heartache.

Chapter Four

Dawson was impressed with the ice skating rink, but he had to admit, he was more impressed with Mikala. She was an attractive sight, clad in black leggings and an oversize teal sweater with a zigzag black stripe. Something inside him made him want to kiss her senseless and not stop there. He wasn't sure what that was.

Shoving those thoughts and visions aside, he concentrated on the open lobby with its fireplace, chair groupings and an almost lodgelike feel. He noticed Luke looking around the area with a fair amount of interest, too.

Mikala motioned to the rink beyond the lobby with its floor-to-ceiling windows and a view of Moonshadow Mountain.

"It's like a resort," Dawson noted. "Did you say Angus McDougall put up the money for this?" Brenna

McDougall's family had always had money, though she'd behaved as down-to-earth as everyone else.

"He started the fund drive with a good sum about six years ago. Groups and organizations ran bake sales and craft fairs and that kind of thing to add to it. He wanted the community to feel as if they were putting in their share, I guess. And I think it worked."

Dawson asked Luke, "What do you think?"

"It's an ice skating rink," his son answered offhandedly, but Dawson saw Luke's gaze go to the rink and the kids and adults of all ages who were skating there.

"Are you game to try it?" Mikala asked Luke.

"Sure, why not. It's not as big as the rink in Phoenix, and the music's lame, but I'll try it."

Dawson and Mikala exchanged a look. The "lame" music came from a speaker system that was playing soft rock in an attempt to appeal to all ages.

"Let's rent skates," Dawson suggested. "If you like coming here, we can get you a pair."

"Whatever," Luke responded and started for the rental desk.

Dawson hoped today was going to go well for Luke. Moving here was all about changing the pattern of their lives…to learn how to be a family with just the two of them. When he thought about the family they'd been, he realized that they'd been lacking in so many ways. That had been his fault. He and Kelly should have gone to counseling and worked on building the intimacy that just hadn't been there all along. Now he wanted good communication to be the cornerstone of his relationship with Luke. But Luke had to be open to it.

Suddenly Dawson caught a citrusy scent as Mikala came up beside him. She leaned close so he could hear her above the music. "Your worry is showing. We're all going to have fun today," she said with enthusiasm that seemed sincere.

"From your mouth to my son's heart. Let's get those skates. I'm ready for a workout." If he concentrated on balance and skating and staying upright, maybe he and Luke could both put aside their angst for an afternoon.

A half hour later, Luke was skating on his own around and around the outskirts of the rink. Dawson had been doing the same at a faster pace. When he stopped, he spotted a game room on the other side of the rental desk with a Plexiglas window. Peering in, he spied a pool table, a Ping Pong table and a couple of video games.

His thoughts shifted back to his son. Wasn't that another kid racing with him? Maybe he really would make friends here.

When Dawson glanced around for Mikala, he was surprised to see her bending over, holding a little girl's hands. The child looked to be about Abby's age. Mikala was helping her keep her feet under her, skating backward herself, pulling the little girl along.

As he skated over to them, he asked, "Who's this?"

"This is Riley O'Rourke's niece, Colleen. She's five and not too steady on her own. Riley asked me if I could keep an eye on her while he took her brother to the men's room."

"Does Riley come here often?"

"With his nieces and nephews. He says he can only handle two at a time, but that's not true. When the town had a barbecue in the park last summer, he had them all around him. They think he's the Pied Piper."

"Is he still the bad boy in town?"

"Not so much. Since he returned to Miners Bluff, I think he leads a quiet life. Did you know he was in the Marines?"

"Really? I can't believe it."

"The year after graduation, he got into some trouble. From what I understand, he had a decent judge who gave him the direction his father couldn't and told him to talk to a recruiter. He did, and he's like a completely different person these days."

"Riley O'Rourke, a Marine. There's something I never thought I'd hear."

A moment later Riley was there, his nephew beside him. His niece carefully let go of Mikala's hands, one at a time, and took hold of her uncle's, gazing up at him adoringly.

Riley looked down at her, his blue eyes sparkling with amusement, his black wavy hair tousled.

Dawson remembered Riley and some of the trouble he'd gotten into—stealing another team's mascot, hiking out into the wilderness to binge-drink with friends…a rough crowd, not the same kids Dawson ran around with. It had taken guts for him to enter the Marines, and Dawson wondered what kind of man he was now.

Riley grinned and shook Dawson's hand. "Hi, Dawson. We didn't get to talk at the reunion. I hear you're back in town for good?"

"We'll see."

"Yeah, I guess I'm still in a settling-in mode, too."

"You're Clay Sullivan's partner now?"

"Yep. And enjoying the work."

"Your family must be glad you're back in Miners Bluff."

"Oh, they're glad all right. So I can be a babysitter. That's what I'm doing today," he said with a chuckle.

"Doesn't look like you mind too much."

"Taking care of them is a cinch after— Let's just say it's easier than what I was doing in the Marines." He grinned as his niece tugged at his arm. "I'd better take them over to the snack bar. It was good to see you again. I'm sure we'll be running into each other around town."

Then Riley was skating away, his niece holding on tightly, as if she trusted him to take her anywhere.

"He's good with kids," Mikala said. "It just comes naturally to some people, I guess."

"I found it was a learned skill," Dawson admitted. "But then I was an only child. Riley had brothers and a sister. He helped with them when he was growing up."

Even though they were standing on ice and cold seemed to imbue the whole room, he didn't feel cold standing by Mikala. He had to wonder if she was experiencing the same sensation…the heat that seemed to invade a room when they were together. Only one way to find out.

"Skate with me," he said, and it was more of a command than a request.

Her eyelashes fluttered and he knew that she was flustered by his invitation. Since he didn't want her thinking about it too long, he slipped his arm around her waist and caught her hand.

She looked up at him with that dark brown gaze that asked so many questions. He didn't have any answers. The only thing he knew was that holding her in his arms was a pleasure, and the idea of kissing her again kept him awake at night. Now, his arm around her, their bodies somewhat nestled together, their gazes held and locked.

"On three," he said, not giving her a chance to back out.

They began gliding together, tentatively at first, then with more confidence.

There'd been a rink in nearby Flagstaff when he was a kid and his parents had signed him up for lessons there on Saturdays. His dad had usually driven him and they'd talked sports and anything else that had entered their heads. Those times with his father had made his parents' cold tension more bearable. Dawson hadn't much cared for the actual lessons, but he'd enjoyed the group skate and had dated some of the girls he met at the rink. He'd dated a lot of girls. He thought about the months he'd dated Kelly. When she'd gotten pregnant and he'd proposed, he'd dreamed of a home and family and a real marriage like his parents *hadn't* had.

But when he'd been with Kelly, he'd never felt the easy familiarity he experienced with Mikala. He'd never felt as disconcerted by the sexual electricity, the desire to kiss her and pull her into his embrace—and never let her go.

Mikala's hand gripped his tighter and he realized if he didn't keep his mind on what he was doing, they'd end up on their butts on the ice.

As they passed other skaters, Mikala seemed determined *not* to lean into him. If she did, his chin would brush the top of her head. Again thoughts of their kiss and how perfectly she'd fit against him came to mind. His imagination ran wild with the other ways they would fit together perfectly if they were naked.

No. *Shouldn't* happen.

As he held her left hand in his right, he could feel her arm loosely surrounding his waist. Her hair, thick and glossy, brushed his chest. Her citrusy scent teased his senses and he felt a surge of arousal that was damn near impossible to will away.

As they moved, a breeze rushed by them, ruffling her hair and pushing it against his cheek. He practically groaned. He could feel Mikala's hand against his jacket and he suddenly realized how much he'd missed touching and being touched.

Mikala is just a friend, he warned himself. But as one song segued into the next, he held her just a little tighter. To his relief she seemed to relax more.

Dawson bent his head and spoke into her ear. "We do this well together."

Mikala turned toward him, her lips not far from his. "Skating with you is as easy as dancing."

He wouldn't call it easy. He'd call it something quite different from that. Her breath hitched a little and he was satisfied to see she was affected by their closeness, too.

Close and enjoying it. That had to be enough.

Watching where they were going, he reinforced his resolve to put Luke first. After all, he'd failed as a dad for years. As Mikala had suggested, he'd made the choice to put work first on too many occasions. Maybe if he hadn't, Luke would be able to trust him enough to confide in him now. Well, he wouldn't fail again. He would put his son first.

Besides, Dawson wasn't looking for a serious relationship—and he wasn't sure he really wanted to get married again. He just wanted to deal with his life the way it was and be a better father to Luke.

Having Mikala in his arms just for a skate wasn't a temptation he should invite in. Yet it was damn hard to let her go. He slowed their pace and guided her toward the side of the rink. "I'd better check on Luke."

As she slipped from his hold, he felt an emptiness he couldn't deny. Their gazes held for a few moments and then she looked away, spotting Luke, who was still on his skates standing over by one of the long windows. He was gazing up at Moonshadow Mountain, its snow-capped peak purple in the dusky light.

"Let me talk to him," Mikala offered. "Maybe I can find out what he's thinking."

Dawson figured that was probably the better way to go for the moment. And later, in the privacy of their suite, maybe he and his son could begin to communicate again.

As Mikala skated toward Luke, she watched Dawson glide toward Riley. He could fit in here again if he wanted to. Hopefully, Luke could too.

As she stopped beside the boy, she didn't try to start a conversation right away. She gazed up at the mountain with him. "It's something to see, isn't it?" she commented after standing there for a while. "I think you'd enjoy hiking up there. Your dad did that a lot with his friends. Hopefully you'll get to meet Clay Sullivan and Zack Decker soon."

Luke just frowned. "I don't know anybody here."

"But you will, especially after you start school."

His scowl became even deeper. "I miss Granddad."

"Did you spend a lot of time with him?"

"On weekends. I wish he was here."

"Maybe he'll come for a visit. And maybe, after you're settled in, your dad will take you to visit him."

"He won't. He doesn't want to go back to Phoenix."

"He wants what's best for you."

Luke didn't respond to that and she watched as he blinked fast to keep emotion at bay, emotion he didn't want anyone to see.

Just like his father.

When Dawson entered the kitchen at the B and B with Mikala and Luke, he was surprised to see Anna sitting with Zack's dad at the kitchen table. Silas Decker was one of the richest men in the state. He'd built up his horse-breeding ranch, the Rocky D, to be nationally renowned. He'd lost weight since his heart attack in the fall. His hair had thinned into a gray halo, and his black mustache was streaked with gray, too. But he looked healthy.

"How was ice skating?" Anna asked the group of them, but focused mostly on Luke.

"It was okay," Luke said.

Anna introduced Silas to Luke as if he were a grownup rather than a ten-year-old. Luke nodded to the older man and started to cross to the counter and the cookie jar.

Silas said, "Your daddy used to ride at my ranch with my son. Darn good rider, too. You ride?"

Luke shook his head. After a moment's hesitancy, he asked, "So my dad was good?"

"Could hold his own. He and his friends rode to Horsethief Canyon and camped there."

Interest shone on Luke's face. "It's a real canyon?"

"Yep. Has a couple of levels and a great floor for

setting up a tent. Maybe in the spring you and your dad would like to go there."

"I've never been camping," Luke admitted, glancing at Dawson.

"There's no reason we can't go," Dawson assured him, liking Luke's interest in the idea.

"My friend Jenny gives riding lessons at the Rocky D. I'm sure she'd take you on if you want to try it," Mikala suggested.

"I'll think about it," Luke said, as if he might. Then to Dawson he asked, "Can I be excused?"

"Sure."

After taking another biscotti from the jar, Luke left to go up to their rooms.

"Fine boy," Silas said. "Looks like you."

"He's got his mother's smile," Dawson said in a quiet voice. He missed Kelly even though their marriage hadn't been perfect, even though growing apart had been painful.

"I'm sorry about your wife," Silas said. "I know what that feels like—to have someone you love suddenly taken away."

Dawson guessed there was a long story there, and he only knew parts of it. One thing he was certain of—Zack hadn't come home for eight long years after his mother's funeral because he'd blamed his dad for her death. But now the two of them seemed to be at peace, and Dawson was glad for them. Their reconciliation made him hopeful that his relationship with Luke could heal.

"It's a harsh deal for Luke to handle and he's having trouble with it," Dawson responded. "But Mikala is working with him and helping already."

"I haven't done anything," she protested.

Dawson knew better than that. "You've done more than you know. Do you think I would have been able to convince him to go ice skating with me today? And when he finally hooked up with those other boys in the game room, he actually seemed to be enjoying himself."

"That wasn't my doing, Dawson. Luke's finding new things to interest him. I can't take credit for that."

Silas rose from his chair. "I think you're all thinking too much. I learned from Zack, you can't force change. Luke will find his way. You'll see. Could be a rough and rocky road, but that's life."

Anna stood with Silas now, looking up at him as if he were someone very special in her life. "I'm going with Silas to the Rocky D. We're watching old movies tonight—*Casablanca, Camelot,* maybe even the original *Pink Panther.*"

"Zack tells me you have a home theater now," Dawson remarked.

"I do. I got it built and set up for Zack's first big movie. He uses it now when he's working and wants to screen rough cuts of his project. You coming over soon?"

"After we get settled in," Dawson promised. "I know Zack just got back from his honeymoon and I don't want to intrude."

"I'm sure he and Jenny would love to see you. We have a rescue horse that they're gentling. Luke might be interested in the process."

"Some weekend when the weather holds. We'll come over and take a look around."

"Luke could pick out a horse he thinks suits him. We've got some great trailblazers."

After Mikala's aunt and Silas left, Dawson asked, "How long have they been dating?"

With her smile, Mikala easily told him she was happy about the idea. "Since Thanksgiving. Jenny asked us over for dinner and we had a great time. My aunt and Silas didn't stop talking. He was still weak then after his heart attack, but seemed to perk up with Aunt Anna there. They went to high school together."

"Then I guess life intervened."

"Yep, sure did. Silas was hell-bent on building up the ranch, getting it back into good financial footing, and then he met Olivia. But now he and Anna are friends again, maybe more."

"Maybe more." He was beginning to realize he and Mikala had always been *more* than friends. His gaze found hers and held. A charged atmosphere filled the kitchen. "Common history is good foundation to build on."

The pulse at Mikala's neck fluttered and his own heart rate sped up. "You mean like Jenny and Zack built on theirs?"

"And Clay and Celeste."

Breaking eye contact and the magnetic pull between them, Mikala went over to the counter. "Can I get you a snack?"

"Mikala, you don't have to get me anything."

They studied each other again…almost warily. Then she said, "I know I don't have to, but you've only been here a day, so you still feel like company."

In spite of good intentions to keep his distance from her, he went over to the counter and stood face-to-face. "I'm not a guest. Luke and I will change our own sheets and keep our rooms straightened up."

"I usually do the cleaning," Mikala responded with amusement in her voice. "Do you want to run the vacuum, too?"

He raised an eyebrow. "Do you think I can't give a vacuum a good spin around a room?"

The smile she gave him this time was wry. "I think it's probably on the bottom of your to-do list."

He gave in to her desire to take care of everyone. Her aunt must have handed down the trait. Or else Mikala had decided caring for others was a way to garner approval and respect. "All right. I can see you think it's part of your job. But you have so many jobs, who can keep track?"

He pulled a glass from the cupboard and went to the refrigerator for chocolate milk. Nostalgia? Maybe.

Meanwhile Mikala went to a deacon's bench sitting beside the kitchen door and pulled out a pair of slippers from the inside compartment. Her leather boots came almost to her knees and he imagined they were too warm for indoor wear.

They made her legs look great, though.

He walked over to her. "Need some help?"

She looked flustered. "Oh, I can do it."

"I'm sure you can."

Their eyes met and in that instant, he saw her need for independence battling with another, more elusive emotion. But this time, she smiled up at him. "But I'll let you be chivalrous again," she joked.

He laughed and got down on one knee before her and took hold of the heel of her boot. Then he yanked gently but firmly, pulling it off. She held on to the top of her long sock, decorated with music notes in various colors. They made him smile.

"What?" she asked.

"So many things about you are a surprise."

"It's surprising that I don't like dull socks?"

He shook his head and shrugged. "Lots of women do."

"I'm *not* lots of women."

That stopped their conversation cold. The air in the kitchen seemed to crackle with the tension between them. There were sparks there that they'd never acted on in high school.

Now, however, they were trying to deny them, trying to act as if they were still just friends. They weren't doing a very good job of it. He took hold of her other boot and pulled, then he set both of them on the floor beside her. She really did look like a teenager in her leggings and colorful socks, with her hair tousled from skating and her cheeks still flushed from the cold.

He sat beside her on the bench, leaned toward her and couldn't help sliding his hand under her hair. "I don't know what's happening between us, Mikala, but it's damn confusing." He wanted to kiss her desperately. He needed to feel her in his arms again. It was such a wrenching elemental need that he really didn't know how to handle it.

"Please don't look at me that way, Dawson," she murmured.

"Like I want to kiss you again?"

"I don't think you *know* what you want."

Those words hit him hard and he pulled away from her. "What's that supposed to mean?"

Hesitating a few moments, she finally answered

him. "Your wife died and your world turned upside down. Luke has had problems since then. You're looking for an escape."

He was silent a long time, thinking about how he'd felt since he'd returned to town. *Was* he using an attraction to Mikala to cover up everything else that was going on inside of him? The unexpectedness of changing his life...his turmoil about Luke?

"When are you going to have another session with Luke?" he asked.

"I'll give him this week at school. Saturday will be good, unless a problem crops up."

"I wouldn't know what to do without a problem a day."

Her smile was slow in coming, but when it did come, it lit up her face. They were back to being Dawson and Mikala—friends. Maybe they could hold on to that label for a while. But sitting here, feeling the heat between them, it didn't seem too likely.

It was almost eleven on Wednesday night when Dawson closed his laptop and went to check on Luke. Luke's door was cracked slightly and Dawson pushed it open. The bedside lamp was still shining but Luke was sound asleep, still wearing his iPod ear buds. He hadn't said much about school this week though Dawson had tried to get him talking. Maybe his son would open up to Mikala when he saw her on Saturday.

Removing the ear buds and taking the iPod from Luke's chest, he set them on the bedside table and looked down at his boy, his heart full of everything he felt for him. Sure, he loved him. But there was something so much bigger than that, too...something that made swallowing difficult. He gently laid his hand on Luke's head for a moment, then turned out the bedside lamp and left the room.

Dawson thought about going downstairs for a snack then reconsidered. Luke still had bad dreams sometimes. He wanted to be there if his son woke up. But the truth was, he missed Mikala. She'd had counseling sessions throughout dinner last night and tonight. There was something he wanted to ask her.

It was late. Would she still be up?

Going to his room, he picked up his cell phone and dialed her number. Half expecting the call to go to voice mail, he was surprised when she answered on the second ring. "Dawson? Is everything okay?"

"Yes. I hope I didn't wake you."

"Oh, no. I just got out of the shower and—" She stopped abruptly.

But that stop made him wonder what she was wearing. A robe? Anything? Was her long hair wet? Or had she gathered it on top of her head as she'd done once in a while in high school?

Thoughts of high school always brought back memories of the prom. He wondered if the self-protective guard Mikala tried to keep securely in place had to do with what had happened that night. Had she blamed herself for the way Carson Simmons had acted? When Dawson had seen her torn prom dress, the terrified look on her face, he'd wanted to smear Carson against the windshield. Instead, he'd roughly pushed him away from Mikala, helped her out of the guy's car, swept her into his arms and carried her to his Mustang. Even though that night had happened so long ago, he remembered it as if the prom had been yesterday.

"I won't hold you up," he assured her. "I just wondered what your schedule looks like the next couple of days. Or maybe the beginning of next week. I'd like to check out a few houses and I wouldn't mind having a second opinion."

With only a slight hesitation, she reminded him, "You're the expert in construction. I wouldn't think you'd need a second opinion." She was fishing for his motive and he *did* have one.

"This isn't just about construction. I'm looking for something different than we had before. Not something with so many rooms Luke and I can't find each other. I want him to feel at home. I guess I want a certain atmosphere about the house, sort of like the Purple Pansy has—that feeling of coming home. I'm not sure walking into an empty house, I'll realize if it has it or not. *You* might."

"You think women are better at that?"

"I think *you* might be better at it." After all, he'd already discovered she was the most intuitive and perceptive woman he'd ever met.

Instead of giving him an answer, she asked, "So how is Luke doing at school?"

"He's not saying much. I ask. He clams up. I helped him with a couple of math problems he seemed frustrated with, then he went to his room and shut me out with those ear buds again."

"Do you know what he's listening to?"

"Yes. He likes a variety of musicians and his apps are still wholesome kid stuff."

"You keep a close watch."

"I do now," he confessed. "You've had long hours this week," he commented.

"Some weeks are like that. But I like what I do and it's my...life."

She needed more of a life than her work. Even *he* knew that. It had taken him many years to learn it, but he had, the hard way.

She went on, "I try to keep a few hours free on Friday afternoons. Do you think you could arrange to look at houses then?"

"I've been in touch with a real-estate agent. I'll call her in the morning."

"I'll be at the elementary school tomorrow," she said. "But if you leave a message on my voice mail, or with Aunt Anna, I'll get it."

"Will do," he agreed. He could keep talking to her all night. But a sense of intimacy was already developing between them and a late-night conversation could light too many fires. "Thanks for agreeing to go with me. You get a good night's sleep."

"I will," she murmured. "Good night, Dawson." She hung up.

He held the phone for a while as if he were holding the sound of her voice. Then he laid it on the bed beside him, still wondering if her hair was wet or dry, if she was wearing a robe or a nightgown, if she was slipping into bed and looking forward to Friday as much as he was.

Chapter Five

Mikala stood in the second house on the Realtor's list, knowing this one was as wrong as the last one she and Dawson had toured. The first one, an old Victorian, had needed so much work that Dawson and Luke couldn't have moved into it for at least six months.

As she followed Dawson into the master suite of this almost brand-new house, she realized she'd looked forward to this afternoon all week. But that fluttery feeling in her stomach when she came anywhere near Dawson carried an alert notice with it—*Be careful!*

The real-estate agent had gone outside to make a call and they'd been left alone to wander so they could get a feel for the place. The woman obviously thought they were a couple.

The house had been staged, and as Dawson glanced around the master suite, the huge king-size bed drew their gazes like the proverbial magnet.

They both looked away.

In quick long strides Dawson went to a closet, opened the door and said, "This house reminds me of the one I left in Fountain Hills. It's even bigger."

The wryness in his voice and the furrow in his brow told her there was emotion under the surface.

He peered inside the walk-in closet. "This would be a spare room in a smaller house. Kelly would have had plenty of room for her—"

Stopping abruptly, he quickly strode toward the bathroom.

Mikala didn't know whether to follow or to stay put. However, her instincts guiding her, she went to stand beside him.

The bathroom was practically as big as a bedroom with its marble steps, raised Jacuzzi tub and double shower. The his and hers towels—white with gold embroidery—made a stark comment, pointing out exactly what Dawson was missing in his life—his wife and Luke's mother.

"Do you like the house?" Mikala asked, just to urge him to talk again.

His answer was practical as well as curt. "It's well constructed. There were some shortcuts in the finish work. I could take care of that."

"But?" she prodded.

"I brought *you* along for the 'but,'" he responded with a slight smile that really wasn't a smile at all. He was definitely hiding something…feelings he didn't want her to see. He added, "What's your take?"

"It's a beautiful house, but it's cold," she said without hesitation.

He pushed his hands into his jeans pockets. "I can

see why you think that. This house isn't so much sitting here waiting for a family, as it's just sitting here showing off."

Thinking that she might have been too blunt, that being with Dawson urged her to be more honest with herself as well as with him, she said, "Maybe you have to imagine it with *your* taste—your paintings on the walls and the kind of furniture you like, rather than what someone picked out because they thought it was neutral enough to fit anyone."

He was already shaking his head. "The rooms are too large. The ceilings are too high. That makes the house formal."

"It *is* in a great neighborhood." She was listing the positives, maybe trying to figure out exactly what Dawson was looking for.

"It's a development with very large houses that just fit on small plots of land. When I sign on with a developer, the architect looks at trying to fit homes into their natural environment. As far as neighborhoods go…" His voice trailed off. Finally he went on, "Neighborhoods mattered to my parents. We moved into the house on Hickory Road when I was ten. My mother was so excited because she thought the neighbors were up and coming or had already arrived."

Mikala remembered where Dawson had lived in a very nice section of town. But he never talked about it much. Back in high school she remembered thinking she'd known very little about his home life. "You lived near Clay, didn't you?"

"Sure did. To have a banker as a neighbor made my mom feel important. All I cared about was that Clay and I would live closer together. We were already friends and being able to run in and out of each other's houses was a kid's dream."

"I didn't realize you were friends before high school."

"Yep, we teamed up early. We didn't start hanging out with Zack until middle school."

Absently Dawson opened the medicine cabinet, closed it again, went to look in the shower, then exited the bathroom into the bedroom once more. Crossing to the bed, he sank down on it. "This house really does remind me too much of our house in Fountain Hills."

There was so much regret and sadness in his voice that Mikala had to go to him. She sat beside him on the beautifully flowered taupe comforter. "What are you thinking about?" she asked softly.

Staring straight ahead at the winter landscape on the wall, Dawson took a little time before answering. "Moving into that Fountain Hills neighborhood mattered to Kelly...and to me, too, I guess. Barrett Construction was taking off and we could live anywhere we wanted. I would have preferred something a little more...rural, but Kelly, like my mom, wanted to live in the right neighborhood with the right people."

Facing Mikala, he explained, "I want something different now. For me and Luke—" He shook his head. "I don't care what neighborhood we live in. I just want him to be happy."

"When you narrow it down, you might want to take him along, keep him involved in the decision-making."

Dawson glanced around again. "You're right about that. But narrowing down choices could take time. This house has a lot going for it, but it's not right for us."

Mikala touched Dawson's arm, then almost wished

she hadn't. There was already a connection between them and any kind of physical move toward each other made that connection seem even stronger. "You'll find the right place. It could just take some looking."

When he was quiet, she asked, "What are you thinking about?"

"I haven't had anyone ask me that in a long while."

Is that why he kept his thoughts and feelings to himself except where Luke was concerned?

Finally he said, "I was thinking of opening a branch of our company here. But I don't know if there's enough business in Miners Bluff to sustain it. I might have to start in Flagstaff—that's if I want to expand. I really don't need more to keep me busy, especially not now. But maybe another company in Miners Bluff could give the town a boost and add jobs where they're needed."

"You think about that kind of thing, don't you?"

"I do."

What were the roots of Barrett Construction? What had happened after Dawson had moved away from Miners Bluff with his mother? Why had his parents split up? They were all questions she still didn't feel comfortable asking.

Sitting close enough to Dawson to feel his body heat, knowing he'd asked her along for more than just a second opinion, she decided to venture into what might be sacred territory. "Tell me about Kelly. About your marriage."

He gave her a quick look, and she thought he was going to shut down. But then he turned back to her with sincerity evident on his face. "We were happy at first, even though we married because of the pregnancy.

Kelly told me she wanted the same things I wanted—a home and family. She'd lost her parents and was on her own when we started dating. She seemed willing to follow me wherever the company led. But I don't think she realized how hard I had to work to make it a success. I don't think she realized that the house, the cars, her jewelry and the neighborhood she wanted to live in came with a cost."

"The long hours you put in."

"Exactly. Even after Luke was born, I was still building the company with Dad, adding more crews, expanding our options so we could survive no matter the economic climate. I think Kelly liked being a mother, but I also think she felt trapped by it. Yet neither of us wanted Luke raised by a nanny. Once Luke was in school, she had more free time but it never seemed to be enough. I don't know. Those last couple of years were…tense."

"You didn't talk about it?"

"Oh, Mikala. Communication in a marriage can get tripped up in so many ways. We concentrated on Luke mostly when we were home, and didn't make enough time for each other."

They sat there in silence. Mikala wanted to ask a lot more yet guessed Dawson had revealed all he was going to.

"So what kind of place do you really want?" she asked, changing the subject back to a more comfortable one. "The real-estate agent could probably help you better if you gave her more than a vague idea."

"You're probably right. But the problem is, I can't describe what I want. I'll know it when I see it."

He was gazing at her in that way he had that was

so intensely personal. And the sparks of desire in his eyes made her feel short of breath.

"Mikala," his voice was husky, almost raw.

She knew what he wanted. But he wouldn't take it, not unless she gave the signal she was willing. They both remembered prom night. They both remembered the other kisses they'd shared. She could see the need in his eyes, feel it in the tension that crackled in the air between them.

She leaned toward him, ever so slightly. His arm came around her. When she turned toward him, her leg brushed his. His face was so close, his lips simply a whisper away.

She could still pull back. She didn't have to let this happen. But she suddenly wanted Dawson's kiss more than she'd ever wanted anything in her life. He made her feel desired, but safe. That was a potent combination.

As his lips came down on hers, she realized their passion was even *more* potent. She felt his blazer against her sweater as she inhaled the musky scent of his cologne. She lost her breath as his tongue breached her lips and he was all she cared about in the world. How crazy was that?

Their kiss became a fiery entity of its own. The tip of his tongue played with hers and she lost the ability to think. She lost her inhibitions. She lost every sense of propriety she'd once possessed.

This is crazy, she thought again.

But even crazy didn't seem to matter. Only the sizzle they were generating. The way she felt in his arms mattered. Their desire became so tantalizing, so feverish that she was hardly aware that he'd laid her down on the bed! He was touching her face, kissing her eyelids, murmuring her name. When she slid her hand under his blazer, she was aroused by the hardness of his stomach, his muscled leanness, his restrained power. Dawson's hand caressed her breast. His touch was teasing and seductive. She loved the way he made her feel.

Suddenly a voice sailed up the stairs. "Mr. Barrett, do you have any questions?"

Mikala froze.

Dawson tore his lips from hers and swore. He cleared his throat and then called down to the real-estate agent. "We're just having a last look around. We'll be right down."

Mikala just wanted to lie there with her eyes closed, and deny the embarrassment she was feeling. But of course that wasn't possible. She told herself no one died of awkwardness. But as she pushed herself to a sitting position and glanced at Dawson as he did the same, she wondered if that was true.

After a few beats of silence, Dawson asked, "Are you all right?"

No, she wasn't all right, but she wouldn't tell *him* that. "I'm fine."

"Mikala—"

"Let's not analyze it," she murmured. Then more to herself than to him confessed, "I can't believe we let ourselves get so carried away."

"I thought we weren't going to analyze it." His tone was dry, maybe even filled with a little wry humor.

But, for her, there was nothing funny about what had happened. Especially as a therapist, she should have known better. "I was just an outlet for you. You were talking about your marriage, some of your regrets, and I was just…here."

His brows furrowed and he almost scowled. "So you think if the real-estate agent had sat on the bed with me, I would have kissed *her?*"

"I didn't mean it that way."

He studied her, then shook his head. "I don't understand you, Mikala. You're a confident, independent woman yet I think part of you is amazed I'm attracted to you. Why is that?"

Why was that, indeed?

When she didn't respond, he asked, "How many serious relationships have you had?"

"I don't want to talk about it here."

"If we don't talk about this here and now, I don't think you'll ever answer me. How many did you have?"

"One."

"When?"

"When I was in college, earning my master's."

"What happened?"

"Dawson—" She found herself sliding away from him, trying to put physical as well as emotional distance between them.

"What happened?" He drew out each word in a determined way that let her know she couldn't evade him.

"He found someone else."

A look came into Dawson's eyes that made her angry. "Don't you dare pity me! Don't tell me you understand what it was like to feel rejected like that unless it happened to *you.*" There was so much passion in her words, she was surprised by her vehemence.

Dawson reached toward her, then thinking better of it, dropped his hand. "How long were you together?"

"A year."

Again that look was in Dawson's eyes and she couldn't stand it. She stood, ready to run downstairs.

But he stood, too, clasped her arm and made her stay. "You don't see pity. Maybe compassion, but there's nothing wrong with that, is there?"

"This—" She motioned to the bed, and to them. "This has no place to go. I have trouble…trusting, and you—you have a son who has to come first. I know better than anybody that a parent has to do that, has to put a child before anything else."

"Because your mother didn't."

"Enough, Dawson! This isn't the time or place."

After a long probing look, he seemed to agree. After all, he was a man in transition. And she didn't know if she'd ever be able to risk giving her heart to anyone again. Dawson could obviously see her turmoil. He didn't probe more and he didn't apologize for what had happened on the bed. They were attracted to each other. They always had been and just hadn't known what to do about it.

He did reach out and touch her then. He brushed a strand of hair from her cheek. "You're a beautiful woman, Mikala. I wish you could see that as easily as everyone else does."

She felt embarrassed again and could feel herself blushing. Turning away from him and his touch, she crossed to the door.

Touring houses with Dawson had become a dangerous proposition.

That evening, Dawson felt churned up. He'd left too much unsettled with Mikala. There had been nothing but silence in the car today as they'd driven back to the B and B. They'd gone their separate ways but he'd still felt connected to her...felt they'd left too much unfinished. Now, with Luke comfortably having dessert with Anna, he had a few minutes to talk to her. Anna had checked Mikala's schedule and she didn't have therapy now, yet she hadn't come to dinner. Because of what had happened?

Before he reached the studio, he heard the piano. He knew the song. It was a ballad from *Les Misérables,* one of Kelly's favorite Broadway shows. The song— "On My Own"—was filled with longing and feelings that went as deep as the soul.

He imagined this song resonated with Mikala. Her mother had pretty much abandoned her and even *he* didn't know the full story behind that. Yes, she'd had her aunt, but when your own mother walks away—

He couldn't imagine it. How had that affected the way Mikala thought about herself? Had she made the child's assumption that her mother's leaving was *her* fault? Had she envisioned her mother coming back day after day, week after week, only to be disappointed over and over? Never felt as if she were enough to bring her mom back?

Mikala hid most of her insecurities, but she certainly had them.

The music coming from the studio took on a haunting quality. The notes expressed so much feeling, so much passion. After their encounter at the house this afternoon, he was sure Mikala had no idea how much untapped passion lay inside of her. He suspected they'd hardly skimmed the surface. Yet in this piano piece, he heard all of Mikala's intensity, everything she didn't express. Mikala was all about maintaining control over everything in her world, maybe because so much had been out of control as she'd grown up. What had happened to her in college? How could a man walk away from a woman like her?

It was a moot point. That guy had hurt her badly. She was still protecting herself from abandonment, even now.

He'd almost reached the flagstone patio in front of the studio when the music stopped. He waited for more. He thought she might start up again, but there was only silence. He knocked on the door.

It took only a few moments, but then she was there, her eyes glistening. Had she been crying while she played?

"Are you all right?"

When she quickly turned away from him, he caught her shoulder and nudged her around. She was still dressed in that wonderfully soft yellow sweater.

"Something's wrong. Tell me what it is."

She brushed a tear from her cheek. "I just got a little...sad."

"Why?"

"My mother sent an email. She's having a show in Paris and attached photos of the models and what they're wearing."

"She's trying to keep you involved in her life?"

"I think she's just trying to show off, feed her ego, allay her guilt. That's what she always does. When I was a kid she'd send a short note with fifty dollars, or tickets to a concert or a bracelet so expensive I'd be afraid to wear it. My mother doesn't understand the first thing about me or about my life. If she did, she'd know a phone call was more important than anything else. She'd know a visit wouldn't replace all the years she was away, but it would help."

Mikala turned toward the music room and went to the piano bench. "Why did you come over, Dawson? You and Luke have the evening to spend together."

"You and I need to talk."

"No, we don't. We forgot about the boundaries today. That's all."

"Boundaries? Mikala." He crossed to the bench, slid onto it and turned to face her. His leg brushed hers, but she didn't move away. The piano keys were before them, but that didn't stop him from reaching over and catching her hand.

But she wouldn't let him delve right into conversation. "Where's Luke?"

"He's with Anna having apple pie." He wasn't used to opening up to anyone, so finding the words to express his thoughts to Mikala was tough. "I understand you have some walls up and that's why you don't date," he said. "I have some of my own. I miss Kelly. I loved her. Still do. But something happened to us along the way. Maybe marrying because she was pregnant was the wrong road to take. Maybe that laid a bad foundation for our marriage. Or maybe we just didn't know how to meld our lives, to compromise over the right things."

After a few heartbeats, she said, "I understand."

"No, I don't think you do. I didn't succeed at what mattered most, being a good husband and father."

"So you're reluctant to get involved again."

"I don't want to hurt you. Luke has to come first."

After a long silence, Mikala said, "Being a good

parent isn't easy. It *is* a full-time job." Then maybe because Dawson had given her a window into his soul, she must have felt as if she wanted to do the same. She asked, "Do you know why my mother left?"

"No."

She hesitated and was obviously reluctant to go on. When he squeezed her hand, she looked up at him with all the naive, innocent vulnerability he'd seen in her on prom night. "She'd met someone at an art class. They left for New York to find their dreams together. David wanted to own a gallery someday. She wanted to be a fashion designer. They were together about five years before they split up. By then she'd entered a design competition and won so she was on her way. She never looked back."

Dawson absolutely didn't know what to say. "Did you understand what was going on?"

"No. I just knew she'd met someone and she loved *him* more than she ever loved *me*. I just knew I wasn't enough to keep her here in Miners Bluff. She didn't want to put me to bed at night, play games with me or watch me learn to ride a horse. She simply didn't care about my life."

Mikala's voice trembled a bit and he could see that even now she was putting up a brave front. Yet inside she was still that abandoned little girl with lots of questions.

All of those questions as well as her experience gave her perceptiveness not many women had. She proved it when she said, "You've completely restructured your life for Luke. He comes first. I understand what it's like when your mother is suddenly gone from your life."

"What happened *after* your mother left? Didn't you stay in contact?"

"I would call her and hear *his* voice instead of hers. Each call became more and more uncomfortable until I didn't call at all. And she was too busy to call me." Mikala slid her hand out of his and laid it in her lap.

Gazing at her, understanding her so much better now, he cupped her chin in his palm and kissed her. It was a soft melding of lips, the gentlest flick of his tongue against hers and then it was done.

Her gaze was troubled as she looked up at him. "I don't know if I should be Luke's therapist. Not with whatever is going on between us."

"I know you haven't had many sessions with Luke yet. But outside of those sessions, he *does* seem to connect with you just when you're around. Do you feel you're the best person to help him?"

She didn't answer right away as she soberly considered his question, and maybe his son's love of music and the trust she'd started to build. "I think I can help him."

"All right. That's settled. And as far as you and I go... Let's just take this one day at a time."

Gazing into her eyes, he saw the same longing he felt whenever he was around her. She repeated, "One day at a time."

"First and foremost, we're friends, Mikala. I think both Luke and I need a friend right now."

He slid to the end of the piano bench, stood and crossed the room, feeling as if something good had finally begun.

Chapter Six

As Dawson drove home from the skating rink on Sunday afternoon, he glanced at Luke. Today they hadn't asked Mikala to join them. Dawson knew he, himself, had to establish a solid bond with Luke. But bonds weren't easy to recapture. Luke had skated, peered out at the mountains, and then skated some more...alone.

Dawson could feel his son's loneliness. He knew what it felt like. When his parents were going through their problems, he hadn't confided in anyone. The kids at school had thought he was cool and had it all together. Of course he hadn't wanted them to think otherwise. His parents had believed they were hiding their problems from him. But he'd heard their low-toned conversations and the arguments that weren't supposed to go beyond the bedroom door. And he'd felt completely isolated.

Until the night of the senior prom when he'd connected with Mikala.

He understood Mikala couldn't tell him anything about the session she'd had with Luke yesterday. But Luke wasn't saying a word, either. Dawson felt as if he were on the outside and didn't know how to remedy that.

Snow had begun falling in earnest right before they'd left the rink. Dawson switched on the windshield wipers as he tried to swipe away the big, fat flakes.

He couldn't stand the silence in the car or the disassociation he felt from his own son. There had been a sign in the game room about hockey tryouts. "Do you think you'd like to play hockey? You could take lessons on Saturday mornings and join the team."

"Maybe," Luke responded, giving his usual one word answer.

"Did you enjoy skating today?"

"It was okay."

Three words. *That's progress,* Dawson decided. "It's good exercise. Maybe we could both get fitted up for cross-country skis. Think you'd like to try that?"

This time all Dawson got was a shrug.

"I want you to find things here that you like to do."

Suddenly a spurt of words came from Luke. "I like looking through Aunt Anna's old pictures and hearing her tell the stories about the mine and all."

"Really?" Anna as well as Mikala had an amazing ability to relate to Luke. Dawson was surprised his son enjoyed Anna's stories as much as her apple pie. "What else?"

"I like playing Mikala's piano. It's got a great sound. She said Aunt Anna used to give piano lessons."

"Would you like to take lessons again?"

"Yeah, I guess. If Aunt Anna could give them to me."

"You don't want Mikala to?"

"I'm already seeing her for...other stuff."

Dawson hesitated. "If you ever want to talk about the other stuff, I'm here."

"There's nothing to talk about," Luke muttered and buttoned his lips up tight as if to prove the point.

Dawson waited, hoping Luke would say something else. He knew better than to push. That was a sure way to silence his son.

The road leading to the rink through the foothills of Moonshadow Mountain consisted of only two lanes. Plowed snow banks along the sides narrowed it further. With the snowfall thick, almost at blizzard proportions now, Dawson stared straight ahead.

Though his attention was divided between the road and Luke, they'd gone a little ways when Luke whispered, "How can you see?"

"The windshield wipers are clearing enough of a space." He dared a longer look at Luke who appeared a little pale. "Are you okay?"

Luke didn't answer.

"Luke, is something wrong? Don't you feel well?"

"I'm fine," Luke responded, but Dawson could tell he wasn't. His hands were clenched into fists and his face was tense in a way a ten-year-old's should never be. This was their first drive in the snow. Kelly had driven in snow or ice or something the night she'd died. Was Luke remembering that event? Should he ask?

"I'm a good driver, Luke. The SUV has four-wheel drive. We're safe on these roads."

Luke gave his father a turmoiled look. "That's what Mom must have thought," he murmured.

If he could have, Dawson would have pulled off the road and pulled his son into a tight embrace. But there was no shoulder with the snow piled up, so he did the next best thing. He reached over and clasped Luke's arm. Luke didn't move and he didn't say anything, either. As the antilock brakes took hold on the curve, Dawson needed to keep two hands on the wheel again.

He drove carefully the rest of the way to the Purple Pansy, wondering if they'd made any progress today at all.

After Luke caught the school bus the following morning, Dawson sat at the kitchen table, his laptop open, his mind on work. The internet connection for his laptop was better down here. After two video conferences, one with his father, and one with a foreman, he turned his attention to the numbers on the balance sheet. Although he was in Miners Bluff, although his father was managing the crews, he intended to stay up to date on every bit of it.

The kitchen door opened and Mikala came in. His heart pounded harder. They hadn't spent any time together since their talk in her studio. He often sat here working so she didn't seem surprised to see him. She motioned toward the coffeepot. "Just back for a refill."

"What are you up to today?" He stood and went over to the coffeepot, bringing his mug with him.

"Catching up on chart work. I take lots of notes in

session and I have to make sure they're legible and in order."

He could feel that powerful tugging toward her again. He was almost used to fighting it now...almost.

They reached for the coffeepot at the same time, their fingers tangling. She pulled back and so did he, but not before something akin to an electric shock jolted them both. It had nothing to do with static electricity.

He might as well tell her about the phone call he'd received from Zack and see how she felt about a party at the Rocky D. "I got a call from Zack last night."

"I got one from Jenny," she admitted.

"About the party?"

"Yes. I think they want to celebrate their wedding all over again and so does Silas."

Mikala went to the fridge, added milk to her coffee, then set it on the counter and looked up at Dawson. "Are you going?"

"I'd like to. I want to wish Zack and Jenny the best. I spoke with Anna this morning after breakfast about going. She said she'd be glad to stay with Luke for the evening. Do you think that will be okay? I don't want him to think I'm deserting him."

Mikala picked up her mug, took a cautious sip, then finally said, "I think it will be good for him to know that you have friends, too. Ask him about it. If he seems okay with the idea, tell him he can reach you at any time on your cell phone. That should give him reassurance if he needs it."

"Solid advice, as usual."

She tilted her head and smiled, the morning light shining through the window emphasizing the glossiness of her black hair. He had a sudden desire to run his fingers through it.

Instead he asked, "Do you want to go together?"

That widened her eyes a little and made her take a quick breath. "You mean catch a ride together?"

That's exactly what he meant, right? "Sure. It would make sense."

She repeated slowly, "Yes, it would make sense."

If she kept looking up at him like that, he was going to kiss her again. Knowing he should keep a safe distance, he poured more coffee and carried his mug to the table. "I'd better get back to work."

She studied him thoughtfully. Had she guessed what he was thinking? What he'd like to do? His bedroom was only two flights away and neither of them was ready for that.

"Did Luke mention our session on Saturday?" she asked.

Surprised she brought it up, he answered, "No. When we went skating, I thought he might. But most of the time he just acted as if I wasn't there."

She let a few thoughtful seconds pass before she set down her mug again. "Can I ask you something personal?"

For her sake or for Luke's? It didn't matter. "Yes."

"Before your wife died, did you feel any of this distance between you and Luke?"

That was a question easily answered. Relieved, he said, "No. Even though I worked a lot, whenever he and I were together, we had fun. We could talk."

Mikala nodded as if that confirmed something in her mind.

To give her another piece of the puzzle, he revealed,

"Yesterday, when we were driving home in the snow, Luke got pale and tensed up. I think he was afraid we'd be in an accident like his mother was."

"Did he say anything?"

He told her about their brief conversation, ending with, "I assured him I was there to listen if he ever wanted to talk about anything."

"Right now, that's all you can do."

"I hate feeling powerless."

"I know."

Mikala *did* know. Not only about his worry over Luke, but about his need to reconnect with old friends. Suddenly Zack and Jenny's party seemed like a terrific idea to him. "I think Luke spending an evening with Anna, and me spending an evening with friends could be good for both of us."

But then he gazed into Mikala's dark brown eyes again and knew a night with friends meant a night with *her*—and he was looking forward to it way too much.

In the Rocky D's immense living room on Saturday evening, Mikala studied a new Western artist's painting Silas Decker had acquired. But when she heard Dawson's deep male laugh, she couldn't keep from looking his way.

Jenny came up beside her. "Your history is showing."

Mikala inhaled slowly then let out the breath as she turned to face her friend. She could feel the heat in her cheeks, and she just hoped Jenny was wrong. "No, what you're seeing is surprise. Dawson hasn't laughed much since he came to Miners Bluff. It's good to hear it."

Jenny glanced toward the group of men—Dawson, Clay, Riley, Noah and Zack, all classmates, not all of them friends in high school but mature enough now to appreciate each other's company.

"You're glowing," Mikala said, changing the direction of the conversation.

"Why shouldn't I be?" Jenny returned. "I'm a very happy newlywed. All of our friends are here tonight as well as a few of Silas's. He misses your aunt but knows she's sitting with Luke." Jenny nodded toward Katie, another former classmate, and Celeste. "We'll have to have a girls day out sometime soon."

Mikala would like that. Being with Jenny and Celeste was like being with sisters. It would be easy to bring Katie into their circle. She'd only returned to Miners Bluff a few months before the reunion.

Silas came into the room then and strode toward the group of men. He laid his hand on his son's shoulder. Zack looked at his dad and smiled.

"Real change there," Mikala noted.

"Which proves it's never too late for a father and son to reconnect," Jenny agreed happily.

Counting on that, Mikala had lots of hope for Dawson and Luke. But there was something holding Luke back from Dawson, and it was more than this move to Miners Bluff. He hadn't said as much, but she could sense it. She just had to figure out what it was…help *him* figure out what it was…then give him the opportunity to express it in his own good time.

She'd used xylophones with him on Saturday, doing a call and response exercise. She'd played a few notes, then he'd played a few notes. He'd caught on quickly. He'd been so intent on not doing anything wrong at first, but finally he'd loosened up and even laughed a couple of times. They were still getting used to each other but he was letting his guard down a little more each session.

"Are you and Dawson here on a date?" Jenny asked, bringing the conversation back to where they'd started.

"Oh, no," Mikala quickly responded. "We just came together because it was convenient."

Jenny gave her one of those girlfriend looks. "Really? Why don't we just see about that."

Jenny had a mischievous glint in her eye and that always worried Mikala.

"Be right back," her friend said with a sly smile.

Mikala wandered to a table that had been set up with hors d'oeuvres. Removing the lid from one of the chafing dishes, she poked a meatball with a toothpick and popped it into her mouth. She hadn't eaten supper. Her stomach had been twisted into knots with the idea of coming here with Dawson. She kept telling herself it wasn't a date, but she'd gotten dressed up as if it *were* a date, taking care with makeup, wearing a fitted turquoise Western-fringed top, skinny black pants and boots. The turquoise and sterling pendant at her neck had been a birthday present from Aunt Anna, and she'd clipped a turquoise barrette in her hair.

She needed to relax, just enjoy the party and the company of her friends.

But when the music started, she turned, searching for Jenny, and found her at the CD player adjusting the volume.

Then it happened…that bit of tummy-somersaulting magic. Her gaze met Dawson's across that room and a little trill rippled up her spine. Something must have happened to Dawson, too, because he started toward her just as Jenny and Zack began dancing in the space allotted. Silas's friends joined in and by the time Dawson reached her, there was nothing to feel self-conscious about as she took his hand and he led her onto the floor.

He didn't hesitate to pull her in. After all, they were old friends, weren't they? Now old friends who'd shared a few mind-boggling kisses. They were at a party so why *shouldn't* they dance?

She could rationalize the moment away or she could look into Dawson's eyes and know a bond was forming between them that was richer and deeper than anything she'd experienced before. She was so aware of Dawson holding her, his fingers on her back, his hand enclosing hers. He was so tall and male and indescribably sexy. Her body seemed to want to melt into his.

He murmured close to her ear, "You really look beautiful tonight. And you smell as good as you look."

She couldn't help but smile at that and she returned honestly, "So do you."

A bit of surprise showed in his eyes and then a crooked grin spread across his lips that took her back to their dance on prom night when possibilities and dreams had been limitless. The melody was slow and romantic and they seemed to lose all sense of time and place. Dawson held her a little tighter and she could feel he was aroused. She remembered every moment of their time on the bed in that staged house, and what had almost happened there.

With those thoughts playing through her mind, she was totally startled when the song ended and an up-tempo tune took its place.

Dawson seemed as shaken out of the time warp as she. He arched his brows. "Would you like a glass of wine?"

"That would be great."

Dawson's hand went to the small of her back as he guided her toward the wet bar. There he poured each of them a glass of white wine and handed one to her. She took it, trying to keep her hand from trembling. He'd always had that effect on her.

As she took a sip, he said, "Zack and his dad seem to be getting along really well."

She looked their way. Faster dances didn't seem to be Zack and Jenny's cup of tea, either. Jenny was speaking to Katie while Zack, Riley and Silas seemed lost in conversation.

"It's great to see, especially after so many years of disharmony between them." The whole town knew that Zack had left the Rocky D to pursue his career in California without Silas's approval.

"My dad and I lost contact for a while."

"You did?" Mikala asked, hoping Dawson would go on.

Dawson nodded to a leather and suede love seat across the room where no one was seated right now. Mikala followed him and sat beside him. As they sank into the leather, their thighs brushed. Dawson didn't move a muscle so she stayed put, enjoying the close feel. He was wearing a steel-gray sweater tonight with a V-neck and a collar. A few hairs curled in that V, and she longed to brush her fingers against them.

"My dad and I lost touch after my mom and I moved to Wisconsin. My family wasn't what it seemed to be, especially not my senior year in high school."

"Every family tries to keep up appearances." She remembered what he'd told her—*appearances count.*

"I suppose so. My parent's marriage wasn't solid before then. That year my dad's lumber company lost so much money he had to file for bankruptcy."

"Oh, Dawson. That had to be so hard."

"It was. Not just financially, but for my dad's pride and for my parents' marriage. They tried to hide everything from me for a while, but of course they couldn't. I don't know how I kept up my grades that year, or acted as senior-class president. I guess I was trying to be the perfect son so they didn't have anything else to worry about."

Dawson had been good at whatever he'd tried. Had he felt if he excelled at everything, life at home would be better? She asked a question she'd wanted to ask ever since Dawson had returned. "What happened after the prom? You left so suddenly."

"The day after our senior prom, my grandfather fell down a flight of stairs. Mom and I drove to Wisconsin and Dad didn't come with us. He went to stay with a friend in Phoenix. He moved around at first and I didn't have an address for two months. We didn't have cell phones then, so it was a while before he was in touch. My mother's the one who told me they were getting a divorce."

Mikala couldn't help but cover Dawson's hand with hers. He squeezed her fingers as he accepted her understanding. "I think my dad was ashamed to be in contact with me. I guess he thought I'd think less of him, or something like that. Of course, I didn't. He was still my father. Once he did call me and we talked, I made sure he knew that."

When Mikala squeezed his hand again, Dawson felt that complete understanding between them he found so rare. "I figured out from our conversations that my dad was great with handling people and was a pro at managing crews. But as far as business management went, he was at a loss. After he was licensed, he tried to start a construction company in Phoenix, but he had trouble getting it off the ground. Numbers were more my thing. I'd always been good at math. I knew the lumber business from tagging along after him as a kid. So I went to school and earned a business degree and apprenticed with a general contractor. Then I joined Dad and took hold of the operational running of the business while he handled the personnel. It worked. After I moved to Phoenix, we were closer than we'd ever been."

He paused for a few moments, then continued, "After I married…he and Kelly didn't get along real well," Dawson admitted. "She always said he was too rough around the edges, and Dad— He once told me he didn't think Kelly would make a great mom. He could never explain exactly why, and he was all wrong about that. When she was with Luke, she was there for him. She might have gotten tired of the day-to-day routine of a mom, but I don't know what woman wouldn't."

What woman wouldn't? A woman who desperately wanted a child of her own, Mikala thought. She'd been coming to that point for the last couple of years. Yet she kept silent.

Dawson let go of her hand and asked, "So I know about your mom. She's a clothes designer. You've never talked about your dad."

After a few moments' hesitation, she decided to let

her walls down a little more. "My dad was a couple of years older than my mom. She was eighteen and he was twenty. But he was a biker and wanted no part of being a father. The summer after I graduated from high school, I tried to find him. Aunt Anna helped me. We found out he'd died in a bar fight a few years before."

This time Dawson was the one giving comfort. He angled toward her. "I'm sorry."

She shook her head. "My father was an ideal, a fantasy, sort of like still believing in Prince Charming. I know there are no fairy tales. But once we were looking, I had hoped for a father-daughter reunion." Now she glanced toward Silas. "If I'm lucky, Silas could end up being my uncle. I think we could have a great friendship."

"Do you think he and your Aunt Anna are serious?"

"I do."

Dawson ran his fingertips over the ends of her hair. Although he was barely touching the strands, she could feel what he was doing, and she felt her body warming, thinking about him touching her in more intimate ways.

The conversation in the room grew louder as more guests arrived. Dawson rose to his feet and held out his hand to her. "Come on. Enough serious talk for one night. It's a party. Let's mingle."

Two hours later, Dawson and Mikala walked to the door of the B and B side by side. All night he'd felt as if this were an odd kind of date. After all, they'd gone to the Rocky D together. They'd danced, spoken with friends and come home together.

They'd made small talk on the ride home—about

who they'd chatted with, what had happened, how everyone had matured. Yet underneath it all, whenever the conversation lagged, whenever his gaze met hers, the air heated and their breathing quickened.

At the kitchen door Dawson said casually, "I had a good time tonight. It seems like forever since I talked and laughed...and danced without worrying about the world crashing in around me and Luke."

"You deserve a break."

"Doesn't everyone?" The end-of-January cold nipped at his cheeks and his nose and his ungloved hands. Yet all he could really feel was the heat he and Mikala seemed to generate. All he could really feel was the deep awareness in his gut every time he was with her.

"You know what I mean," she said, looking up at him with those beautiful brown eyes.

"You think I have to give myself permission to relax?"

"I can tell you've been reading self-help books," she teased with a laugh.

He chuckled. "Who knows? Meditation could be in my future."

"I think music is a form of meditation—at least it is for me. When I'm playing an instrument or getting involved in a song, I let everything else fall away. I think that happens with Luke, too. That's why he's always listening to his iPod and likes to play the piano."

"I didn't ask you about your last session with him."

"I'm proud of you," she joked again. Then more seriously, she offered, "He's starting to open up more, Dawson, and physically shaking off some tension. That's a start."

For him, so much had begun with conversation with Mikala. His final decision to move here had been rooted in their exchange at the reunion. "Why do you stay in Miners Bluff?" he asked.

Her cheeks were becoming pink with cold. "For the same reason I listen to music, I guess."

That perplexed him, and she could obviously see that.

"I can set my own pace here. If I had a practice in a city, I'm afraid it would overtake me. My work would control me."

"Why do you think that?"

"I can tell when I speak at conferences, or when I'm invited to colleges to give workshops. I almost become a different person. I get so hyped by the atmosphere, the excitement of talking to others about what I do, a chance to teach the benefits of music therapy, that I go from morning to night without a break. There is such a need for music therapy—with autistic children, with Alzheimer's patients, with end-of-life situations—that the need for what I do could become overwhelming someplace other than here."

"You know yourself."

"I know my limits, though that's not the only reason I stay. Aunt Anna is the biggest reason. I would *never* leave her. She never left me. She's the only one who didn't." Suddenly Mikala turned away as if she regretted saying too much.

But he clasped her shoulder and nudged her toward him. "I imagine your aunt would say you have to find your own life with or without her."

This time when Mikala gazed into his eyes, there was a hint of vulnerability there. "Yes, that's what she'd say. But she's getting older and even if her relationship with Silas works out, I'd still stay here. I owe her so much, Dawson, and I don't want her to ever worry that I won't be here when she needs me."

The emotion in Mikala's voice made *his* throat tighten because he understood how she felt. His own dad was that important to him, too. Leaving Phoenix was the toughest decision he'd ever made.

Getting lost in Mikala's eyes was like going back in time. And kissing her... He'd always laughed at the idea of fireworks exploding whenever two people kissed, but when he kissed Mikala, that was exactly what happened.

He slid his hand under her hair and cupped the back of her head. When she didn't protest, he leaned in and lowered his lips to hers. The tip of his tongue had just touched hers when a brighter light went on in the kitchen and poured through the curtained window.

Curbing any intentions he had of taking the kiss deeper, or making it wetter, of shaking up his libido even further, he drew back and dropped his arms to his sides.

Mikala looked surprised and disappointed for a moment but then she saw the light, too. She checked her watch. "I thought Luke might be in bed."

"It's ten. He should be. Maybe Aunt Anna's being lenient. Come on. Let's find out."

Dawson opened the door, and they stepped into the kitchen. But Luke wasn't in sight. They only saw Anna rummaging in the cheese keeper in the refrigerator.

She glanced at the two of them, took a package of cheese from the drawer and set it on the counter. "Luke and I were getting ready for bed when we decided we were a little hungry. So I told him I'd bring up some cheese and crackers. How was the party?"

"It was great," they said in unison.

"Hmmmm," Aunt Anna intoned. "Many people there?"

"About twenty, twenty-five," Mikala said. "Lots of our classmates and friends of Silas. Jenny said he missed you."

Her aunt looked a little flustered. "Oh, I think that's her imagination running rampant." She pulled a box of crackers from the cupboard. "Luke asked me a question earlier tonight and I thought you two should be aware of it."

"What question?" Dawson felt worry taking hold of him again.

"He asked me if I thought you two liked each other...a lot."

"Aunt Anna—" Mikala began.

Her aunt held up a hand. "You don't owe me any explanations. Both of you realize Luke is a smart boy. I just think you should be honest with him about whatever is going on. Just my two cents, for what it's worth." She picked up the package of cheese and the crackers, said, "I'll see you upstairs," then exited the kitchen.

Thinking about what had just happened outside, Dawson rubbed his upper lip and spotted the lipstick smear on his finger...a smear that Anna had probably spotted. "It's not as if we see each other every day," he said.

"No, it's not, but I think—" Mikala stopped.

"Tell me," he prompted.

"I think we just need to lead separate lives for a little while. It'll be best for all of us."

If he knew what was best for all of them, he wouldn't feel as if the rug had been pulled out from under him. Yet he realized Mikala was right. Luke had enough to deal with. He didn't need to be confused by whatever was happening between the two of them.

"You're right, of course." So instead of taking her into his arms and kissing her as he longed to again, he reluctantly said good-night and walked away.

Chapter Seven

Two weeks later Mikala watched Luke as he beat on a Native American drum. They'd watched a short video of singers using them and then Mikala had asked Luke if he'd like to play one. She'd switched on flute music in the background and he was pounding in rhythm with it, expressing himself, letting emotion out. He needed outlets for everything he was feeling and couldn't talk about…yet.

"I can't really play," he muttered for more than the first time as he stopped.

"You're doing great!"

"Why are you watching me?"

"Does that bother you?"

When she turned off the music, he seemed disconcerted with the silence. But then he answered, "I don't know. I guess not, as long as you don't care how I do it."

"I care, but not like a teacher watching a student. I'm just interested in what your feelings have to say."

At that, his gaze met hers. "My feelings don't talk."

"They're coming out in your drumming. And feelings can be expressed in lots of ways—the words we use, the gestures we make—like if you push somebody when you're mad, in the colors you pick when you draw, in the way you drum."

"Can we do something else now?"

"Sure. Would you like to play a song from the sheet music you brought?"

"I guess. But can I ask you something first?"

"Yes, you can."

"Why don't you and my dad talk anymore?"

Uh-oh. The session was supposed to focus on Luke, but she supposed her relationship with Dawson was part of his life now.

"Did you have a fight?" he wanted to know.

Whatever Luke was imagining in his mind was probably worse than what she and Dawson had decided. Better be honest with him. "You know that your dad and I knew each other when we were in high school, right?"

Luke nodded.

"And since you and he moved to Miners Bluff, your dad and I have become friends again."

"Yeah, you guys seemed to have fun when we went ice skating."

"We did. But your dad and I thought it would be better for you if we keep to ourselves for now. Your dad brought you here to try to figure out what's best for both of you, to try to help you be happy again, whether you remember what happened or not."

"I think he wants me to remember."

"Maybe he does. But if he does, I think he wants you to remember for *your* sake so that you don't always wonder about it."

Luke thought about that, then he asked, "So why can't the two of you be friends?"

"He wants to concentrate on why he brought you here, and I want to concentrate on helping you. So that's what we're doing."

"You don't have time to see each other?"

"We're both busy."

Luke swung his legs back and forth for a few moments then met her gaze. "I know Dad always worries about me. But since he doesn't spend any time talking to you, he's...different."

"Different how?"

"Not grumpy, because he tries to be really patient with me. I guess he's afraid I'll run away again. But he's—"

Mikala had something that would help in exactly a situation like this. She pointed to the wall at a small poster. There were blocks all over the poster with all kinds of faces and actions. Under each different picture was a word, labeling the emotion the picture depicted.

She pointed to the poster. "Why don't you take a look at this chart and find the picture and word that matches the way you think your dad is feeling."

Luke spent some time studying the chart. Finally he put his finger on a picture of a man pacing a room. Underneath the picture was the word *restless*.

"So you think he's restless?"

"Maybe. Or maybe this one." This time Luke had

chosen the face of a man who wasn't scowling, but close to it. The word underneath was *frustrated*.

"I see. So you think restless and frustrated might describe your dad?"

"Yeah, but only when he thinks I'm not looking." Luke hesitated. "I think he misses you."

Could that possibly be so? Mikala was flustered by the certainty in Luke's tone.

"How would you feel about asking your dad what's bothering him?"

"I can't do that."

"Why not?"

"I just can't."

There was finality in Luke's words that told her he wasn't going to change his mind anytime soon. She had to get to the bottom of why he wouldn't talk to Dawson about anything important, and she had to do it so they could both move on.

While Mikala met with Luke, Dawson agreed to an early dinner with Clay and Zack at the Shamrock Grill. Dawson waved to Liam O'Rourke, Riley's father, behind the cashier's desk, then scouted the restaurant for his two friends. They were easy to spot, both taller than the average men seated in the tan booths and at the wood tables. Dawson's height matched theirs and when the three of them played basketball, they were all murder to guard. Dawson wished he could keep his mind on basketball, or even his dinner. This was supposed to be a break from the worry he always felt when Luke met with Mikala.

The guys motioned him to the seat across from them.

"The special's Irish stew tonight," Clay said with a wide smile. "You won't get any better."

"Is that what you're having?" he asked them.

"Zack's thinking about the meat loaf and mashed potatoes," Clay said. "I'm still wavering."

Once they'd decided on dinner, the waiter took their orders.

"Riley told me he eats here a couple of nights a week," Clay said, speaking of his new partner.

"His dad seems to be doing well now," Zack commented, glancing at Liam. "I can remember all those years ago how tough life was for Riley when Angus McDougall forced Liam to close the restaurant. No kid should have to go through the chain of events they did."

"Riley was tough then and still is," Dawson said. "His stint in the Marines couldn't have been easy."

"He was in Iraq and Afghanistan," Clay revealed. "But he seems to have come through it okay. He said he just wants peace and quiet now."

"Except when he's with his family," Zack added with a chuckle. "Two brothers, a sister, and nieces and nephews don't a quiet reunion make."

"I was surprised when I saw him dancing with Brenna McDougall at the reunion," Dawson remarked. "Maybe their families have put their feud in the past."

"Or not," Zack said. "Riley won't talk about Brenna or the reunion."

"Our reunion set a lot of things in motion." Dawson thought about Mikala again and every kiss they'd indulged in. He'd missed her the past two weeks…missed her smile and her quiet laugh and easy way she had of putting everything in perspective.

"So how are you and Luke?" Zack asked, looking

as if he wanted an honest answer. Zack always could see through almost any situation.

"The whole process is slow," Dawson admitted. "We've been ice skating a few times and he seems to like that. I'm not sure about school. He won't talk about it. I don't know if he's really making friends."

"That takes time," Zack assured him. "And guys form groups that are hard to break into, just like girls."

"Speaking of girls…" Clay drawled. "You and Mikala looked as if you were having a good time at the party…especially when you were dancing."

A good time. Dawson wasn't sure that summed it up. "We did."

"But…?" Clay asked.

"But she's treating Luke and I'm concentrating on what he needs right now."

"If you don't want to get serious with Mikala, you shouldn't start anything," Zack advised. "She's pretty special. And I think she's been hurt more than she wants to admit, starting with the night of the prom. But you'd know all about that."

"I never realized the whole town knew about that," Dawson muttered.

"Not the whole town. Maybe you didn't notice because you were so involved with what was happening, but there *were* witnesses. I came out in time to see you take Mikala to your car. And Carson… He was persona non grata after that. Whether Mikala knew it or not, lots of kids respected her."

"I wish—" Dawson started, then stopped.

"Wish what?" Clay asked.

"I wish I would have stayed in Miners Bluff. I think my life might have been different if I'd stayed."

"And started something with Mikala?" Zack asked.

"Yes." There, he'd finally said it. But on the other hand… "The thing is—if I'd have stayed, I wouldn't have married Kelly and had Luke. We have problems now, but I can't imagine my life without him."

The men were silent for a few minutes, each lost in their own thoughts.

After their waiter brought their orders, Clay asked, "How would you like to do something different with Luke?"

"How different?" Dawson asked warily.

Clay broke into a laugh. "Only different enough to have fun. How about tubing on the snow in my backyard tomorrow? We've got a few hills. I think he'd enjoy it."

"I'll ask Luke and get back to you."

She hadn't been able to refuse.

Mikala stood at the top of the hill above Clay's backyard, dragging her tube behind her. About an hour ago Luke and Dawson had come to the door of her studio.

Luke had looked up at her and asked, "Do you want to go tubing with us?" Dawson had just given her one of his irresistible smiles. And to rationalize, she figured an afternoon of outdoor fun could help open communication between father and son. Coming along had little to do with wanting to be with Dawson again. Right?

Wrong, said a tiny voice inside her.

Suddenly Dawson was by her side. She knew it was him because of the awareness she felt, the hairs on her neck prickling, the flare of heat rushing through her body.

Dawson motioned to Luke. "He seems to be having fun."

Luke was sliding over the hillocks on his tube and the several times he'd climbed back up the hill, he'd worn a grin on his face. It was so good to see him smiling.

"I think he likes Clay and Celeste, and he's good with Abby."

"She took to him as if he was her older brother."

"That's good for him—to be looked up to."

"I've missed talking with you."

Turning toward him now, full face, Mikala gazed up into Dawson's eyes and wondered if that was all he'd missed. But she could see there the same knowledge that she had of him. When they kissed, the earth moved. He missed more than talking and so did she. They both knew it.

"So what do you think about a toboggan ride?" he asked.

She stared at the toboggan which was made of basswood and willow. It was old-fashioned but looked sturdy, too. "Is that an antique?" she asked with a quick smile.

"You'd have to ask Clay that. But even if it is, it's in good shape. I wouldn't let you ride on anything that was unsafe."

No, he wouldn't. But riding with him could be unsafe for other reasons. "Would I be in front or back?"

"You'd be in front but I can still steer. It can be a little tricky to control the weight and motion."

She had no qualms about letting him be in control. "All right. I'm game. Let's see if old is better than new."

As Dawson pulled the toboggan up beside them, she asked him, "So how's work going? Are you able to keep up with everything?"

"Dad's a great help. He supervises the crews and then I just have to choose new projects and keep on top of the financial aspect of running the business. I'd actually like Dad to move up here with us."

"What would your dad do if he lived up here?"

"He'd be my right-hand man in a new branch of our construction company."

"So you're seriously thinking about this?"

"I am. I drove around Miners Bluff and Flagstaff. There's a lot to be said for bringing the business to the area. With Flagstaff being a college town, there are lots of new ideas, new developments, new housing for people to live in. We're heading into an upswing and I think this is a good place to be, maybe even better than Phoenix. Instead of a gated community or an apartment complex, we can concentrate on individual houses, quality homes with decent pricing in Flagstaff as well as Miners Bluff."

"Are you ready to start something new now?"

"Whether I'm ready or not, I have to build a life here for me and Luke. I won't work the hours I once did. But I want him to understand that working hard at something is the best way to get ahead."

"In other words, you want to teach him what life's all about by example."

"Exactly. If we can get through all these changes together, then he'll learn he can get through anything."

Dawson's philosophy was sound. He was a good

dad. But was he missing something Luke was trying to tell him? Was *she* missing something?

Luke was down at the bottom of the hill near the house watching Abby make snow angels. As Celeste joined her daughter, Mikala heard the laughter that floated up to them.

Dawson watched as Clay finished a slide down the hill in a tube and joined his wife and daughter. "They're a real family," Dawson said.

Mikala heard the regret in his voice for the family *he'd* once had. "They've become a real family since July. Before that, Zoie and Clay weren't talking and hadn't seen each other since the divorce. Celeste felt like a distant aunt. But then she returned for the reunion and everything changed. She'd always wanted to be a part of her daughter's life and last summer seemed to be the right time. But Clay had to agree. Obviously he *more* than agreed."

"Clay told me they all actually get along," Dawson remarked.

"They do. Zoie doesn't try to be Abby's mother now. *She's* the favorite aunt and it works. Abby loves to have fun with her, but at the end of the day, Zoie can leave and the responsibility isn't hers. That's always been the way she looks at life, and Clay finally realized it."

"Zoie always liked exotic things," Dawson said with a chuckle. "And Celeste just wanted a home."

"Maybe they've both found their bliss."

"Yep. And maybe we'll find ours on this toboggan," he joked.

He straddled it and sat, then waited for Mikala to do the same. She was nervous and anxious and self-conscious and every other adjective she could think of, but she sank down in front of him and, tilting a little, ended up balanced on his thighs.

"Sorry," she said, scrambling forward.

He caught her around the waist. "Don't go too far. We have to sit tight together so our weight gives the toboggan the momentum."

She was between his legs now, feeling very unsettled. She'd worn her down jacket and ski pants, so it wasn't as if there wasn't enough padding between them. Yet when his arms came around her, that padding seemed like nothing at all. The heat of his body radiated through the nylon and feathers. His strong arms wrapped around her waist as he held the cords. His long legs were beside hers. She could feel him surrounding her.

"Maybe this wasn't such a good idea," she murmured, more to herself than to him.

Dawson seemed to hear everything whether it was out loud or in her head. "Relax, Mikala. This will be fun." He held her a little tighter. "Get ready for the ride of your life."

Seeing they were ready for a run, Clay clomped toward them at the top of the hill. Dropping the lead to his tube, he said, "I'll give you a push."

Dawson waved his agreement.

"Ready?" Clay asked.

Dawson motioned him to go ahead and Mikala held her breath.

Clay came up behind the toboggan, ran with it a little and gave it a giant push over the top of the hill.

Mikala yelped with the sensation of speeding down the huge hill, her stomach doing flip-flops. Not just because of their speed, but because Dawson was holding her. Pressed against his body, she could feel his arousal and knew he was very aware of her assets. His arms pressed against her breasts as he surrounded her, cocooned her, kept her safe.

Then suddenly, they weren't quite safe. They hit a sheen of ice that turned the side of the toboggan and veered them in a different direction. Dawson fought for control but only managed to steer them over another icy patch that pushed them sliding toward a stand of trees.

Luke shouted, "Watch out, Dad!"

Mikala could hear the trembling fear in the boy's voice.

Fighting for control of the toboggan, Dawson only managed to shout, "We're fine," before they skidded and slid into a pile of snow that was a throw-away zone for the path carved out to stomp up the hill.

Luke ran in the deep snow most of the way up the hill until he got to them. "Are you all right? Dad? Mikala?"

"Just a little shaken up," she assured him, then she looked at Dawson.

Dawson wore a scowl. "I'm fine. That was a stupid move on my part. I should have been able to steer better."

But none of that calmed Luke. "You could have run right into that tree. You could have hit your heads. You could have...died." He looked absolutely stricken.

Dawson didn't hesitate to go to his son and wrap his arms around him.

But Luke wriggled out of his arms and shoved him away. "Go away! I don't need that. I don't need *you*." Tramping down the hill, he stopped only when he took

hold of his tube and walked away from the house...
away from them.

"He's afraid of losing me, too." Dawson's voice was
pained. "I don't know how to reassure him when he
won't let me get close."

"Do you want me to talk to him?"

"Let me try first."

She heard the longing in Dawson's voice to be the
one to help his son. After all, she was really an out-
sider. He didn't want to rely on her. Yet that's why he'd
brought Luke to her.

She waited while Dawson went to Luke, while he
dropped his arm around his son's shoulders. But no
sooner had Dawson said something, than Luke pulled
away, obviously upset. Dawson didn't move after him.
She understood he didn't want to make his son run
even farther from him. She ached for Dawson and all
the turmoil inside of him. She ached for Luke and all
he was going through.

Could she help? Or would she just make matters
worse? Here in Clay's backyard, they didn't have the
privacy her studio would provide. Here in Clay's backyard, there was more distraction.

Luke sank down into the snow and just sat there.
She could see the swell of emotion on Dawson's face,
the desire to go to his son again and his fear he'd make
matters worse. His gaze met Mikala's and he gave a
nod. It was permission to do what she could.

Mikala made her way through the snow toward
Luke, knowing whatever emotions had risen up in him
needed to be expressed—the sooner the better. When
she reached the ten-year-old, she sank down onto the

snow beside him, keeping a little space between them, not saying a word.

Finally he said, "Dad's mad at me."

"Why do you think that?"

"I pushed him away."

"I don't think he's mad at you. I think he's worried about you."

Luke glanced over his shoulder and saw Dawson dragging the toboggan toward the house. Then he cut a quick glance to Mikala and said, "When you and Dad fell off the toboggan, it was like—"

He sounded as if he were choking on his words and Mikala knew this was serious. "Tell me," she encouraged with what she hoped was a no-pressure tone.

"I...I remembered the windshield breaking. I felt the car spin and roll." There were tears in his voice now.

"And I heard Mom cry." His words were lower but Mikala could still hear them. They ended on a little sob that broke her heart.

She moved closer to him in the snow, let her arm brush his. "Whatever you're feeling is okay. Whatever you're seeing we'll make sense of." When she put her arm around his shoulders for comfort, he didn't shift away.

Each of his tears seemed to fall into her heart, burning, and hurting her, too. She sat there with Luke like that until his chest stopped heaving. Snow began falling, frosting the already white landscape. Slowly, Luke's grief ebbed and finally he pulled away.

"I don't see anything else," he said almost angrily. "I don't *hear* anything else. I can't remember. I just can't, no matter how much Dad wants me to. I can't remember what happened *before* we went off the road."

It wasn't that he couldn't, Mikala believed now. His subconscious wouldn't let him.

"You *are* remembering. It's very important that you share what you're remembering with someone, if not your dad, then with me or even with Aunt Anna. If you remember when you're with one of us, just say so and we'll help you."

"What if it happens at school? What if I…cry?" He swiped the wetness from his cheeks as if tears were totally unacceptable.

"You can ask to be excused and go to the bathroom. Or you can ask your teacher to call me, or your dad. It's okay if you do that. Your dad can make sure your teacher knows that's what she should do."

"But what about the other kids? They'll think I'm weird!"

"The other kids don't have to know. You have lots of choices, Luke. You can decide what you need and who you want to tell. But one thing I want you to know above all else—you do *not* have to deal with this alone."

He studied her, searching her face. "Do you think I'll remember more?" He almost sounded fearful of that, but he wanted her to be honest, too.

"I don't know. You might. It could happen in a couple of days, a couple of weeks, a couple of months. But I don't want you to be afraid of it. If you *do* remember, we'll talk about whatever happens. We'll get through it."

He kept staring down into the snow as if it could bury his memories, bury feelings he wasn't ready to deal with. After sitting there a few more minutes, eventually he did turn toward her. "I'm glad you were here today."

"I'm glad I was, too."

After another pause, he shifted away from her. "I'm getting cold."

"Me, too. Have you had enough tubing for today?"

"Yeah, it was fun until…until you and Dad spilled. Are you going to tell him what I remembered?"

"That's up to you. Do you want to tell him? Or would you like me to tell him? Would you like us to all sit together and talk?"

He thought about it. "Can you just tell him for now? I don't want to."

"For now." They both stood and she settled her hands on Luke's shoulders. "You know your dad loves you, right?"

Luke nodded.

"At some point we all have to talk. I just want you to think about that, okay?"

He nodded again.

They started walking toward the back porch where Dawson was standing all alone. She knew how isolated he felt. She wished she could make him feel less so. But that could get them both into big trouble. Consoling Dawson was dangerous territory she didn't want to barge into right now. Consoling Dawson could turn into kissing Dawson, could turn into making love with Dawson. She couldn't let that happen. It was too soon for him and possibly too late for her.

Mikala headed for the Purple Pansy's detached garage on her way to a group-home session. She couldn't help thinking about what had happened with Luke when they'd gone tubing a few days ago. During their sessions she hoped she was giving him confidence to share what he was thinking, whether in music or just by talking to another person. She hoped she was teaching him that he had options and could make choices without someone's approval being the motive for them. Luke had to know he had a say in his life and could express it in lots of ways.

Her boots made distinct footprints in the fresh snow that had fallen last night. She'd almost reached the side door of the garage when an SUV turned into the B and B's parking lot. Turning, she watched Dawson park. He spotted her immediately as he exited his vehicle. She remembered how stoic but lonely he'd looked on Clay's back porch. She remembered exactly how his body had felt against hers as she'd settled on the toboggan in front of him.

He didn't look stoic now. He was smiling as he approached her. "Happy Valentine's Day!"

She'd done her best to forget about the hearts and flowers day. After all, she was practical. She knew an expression of love on Valentine's Day might not last through the year. Unless it was from her aunt.

She smiled back. "Happy Valentine's Day to you, too."

There it was again, darn it…that terrific magnetic pull toward Dawson…the glint in his eyes that he felt it, too.

"Are you doing anything special today?" he asked.

"No. I have sessions from now through this evening."

"You won't be home for dinner?"

"Not tonight." Had she subconsciously arranged

her schedule that way? Didn't want to think about
Valentine's Day as she sat across the table from Dawson imagining kissing him again…maybe doing a lot
more than kissing?

He seemed to digest that. Then he took a few steps
closer. "Do you ever celebrate Valentine's Day?"

"You mean with chocolate and flowers? I left that
behind a long time ago."

He was right there then. So close their breaths min-
gled into one white puff. His voice was low and a little
gravelly when he said, "I think you should celebrate
just a little."

"Celebrate how?"

His large hands were warm on her cheeks as he held
her face and gazed into her eyes.

Her heart was racing now as he tipped up her head,
bringing his lips to hers, and she knew in the deepest
recesses of her heart that she was falling in love. Her
feelings for Dawson were becoming too big to man-
age or to keep tamped down.

His kiss became the embodiment of Valentine's
Day. Yet she feared love wasn't in his vocabulary now.
She was afraid all Valentine's Day meant to him was
passion. With Dawson's return to Miners Bluff, she
certainly had found *her* passion.

When the kiss was over, she didn't know what to
do. But she didn't have to do anything because he said,
"I won't keep you. I guess I just wanted you to know
how much I appreciate you."

Appreciate her work with Luke? Appreciate her desire for him? Appreciate that their friendship was definitely taking a turn into something more potent?

Dawson brushed his thumb over her lips and then backed away. So he didn't kiss her again?

After a last irresistible smile, he gave a wave and walked up the path to the B and B.

She went into the garage, confused by the turmoil his kiss had caused.

Chapter Eight

The following Saturday Mikala stared at the package on her desk in her studio and swallowed hard. Removing a pair of scissors from her desk drawer, she snipped the tape along the edges and opened the lid. She was staring at the wrapped package inside when there was a knock at her studio door.

"Come in," she called automatically.

Dawson opened her door, and as always, her heart leapt when she saw him. A joyful feeling inside had her sending him a smile as she remembered his Valentine's Day kiss.

He smiled back, started to say, "I have someone—"

But Luke said from behind him, "Granddad is here. I want you to meet him."

Dawson shrugged. "I hope we're not barging in on anything."

She left her desk and motioned them all in. A man

not quite as tall as Dawson, but who had the same strong jaw, the same high forehead and the same patrician nose came in behind his son with his hand on Luke's shoulder.

His gaze ran over the studio, then up and down Mikala in an assessing way. He extended his hand. "I've heard a lot about you, Miss Conti. It's good to meet you."

"It's good to meet you, too. Is this a surprise visit?"

"I called Dawson last night, told him I could get away for a couple of days. So I surprised Luke this morning."

"Granddad and I are going to spend the whole afternoon together, just the two of us!"

When Mikala searched Dawson's face, she saw that he didn't seem upset. He obviously understood the bond between grandfather and grandson. If he felt left out, he wasn't going to show it.

"What are you going to do today?" Mikala asked Luke.

"I'm going to show him the ice skating rink, then we're going to the movies and then we're going for Chinese food."

"You've got the day planned. Sounds good."

"Can we go now?" Luke asked his grandfather.

"I don't want to cut this short," Dawson's father said in apology.

Mikala was quick to jump in. "I know how much Luke likes spending time with you. Have fun."

After the two of them left, Dawson came over to Mikala and sat on the corner of her desk. "Luke's almost a different kid when Dad's around. It's great to see. I just wish he could be that way with me."

"It's getting better, isn't it?" Mikala had seen changes between Dawson and Luke since they'd arrived and she hoped he could see the progress, too.

"Yes. He does talk to me sometimes now, but not about the important stuff."

"You'd be surprised what's important to a ten-year-old."

"Maybe so." Dawson nodded to the package on Mikala's desk that was wrapped in silver with a glittery white and silver bow. "What's that?"

His gaze held curiosity and a little more. Did he think the present could be from someone important to her? "It's from my mother."

"You don't sound as if that's a *good* thing."

"I'm almost afraid to open it. This is probably something from her spring line."

"So open it and see what you think," he suggested. "I'll be glad to give you a second opinion."

At first she hesitated. Then she thought, *Why not open it with Dawson here? What did it matter?*

It was hard not to look at him while she untied the ribbon and then tore off the paper. Her gaze always seemed to be drawn to his. Yet as it was, the electricity she felt was scary in its intensity. Did he feel that, too? Why was it ratcheting up instead of lessening?

Tearing her gaze from his, she lifted off the lid of the box and brushed back the tissue paper. The first piece Mikala lifted out was a lime green top made of a fabric that she knew would fit like a second skin. The neckline was edged with just a wisp of white lace. The skirt that accompanied it was very short, flouncy and flowered. At the bottom of the box she found platform sandals about four inches high. The shoe was strappy with a large red flower in the center.

A piece of paper tucked into one shoe read: *Thought you might enjoy these. T.* T for Teresa, not Mom.

Just *what* had Mikala expected? A loving note? A wish-I-could-be-there-with-you, or wish-you-could-be-here-with-me? *Get over it,* she told herself for the gazillionth time. *Your mother left you behind long ago.*

She didn't let anything show. She *never* let anything show.

"Try them on for me," Dawson suggested.

"They're summer clothes and it's below freezing outside," she joked.

He motioned toward the fireplace. "It's warm enough in here. Humor me. Try them on."

There was a note of challenge in his tone and Mikala suddenly wondered if he thought her clothes were too conservative. They were sedate for her occupation—businesslike when they had to be, but still—

She accepted his challenge, feeling unnerved by the arrival of the package, even more unsettled by the look in Dawson's eyes as he imagined her in those clothes. On the other hand, she wanted to know exactly what he thought.

Taking the clothes with her into the other room, she shut the door.

Five minutes later, eager to just get the experiment over with, she emerged into the office again and watched Dawson's smile transform into a wide grin.

"Wow!" was all he said.

The top indeed clung and the V neckline dipped into her cleavage. The hem of the skirt landed mid-thigh and the shoes made her feel like a little girl in her mother's dress-up clothes.

"Don't tell me you like this," she said a bit breathlessly as he came closer to her.

"I think I'd like anything you wore. But this—" He waved at her from shoulder to shoe. "This is hot."

She knew her face was probably beet red. "I'm not hot," she murmured.

His grin vanished and he frowned. "Why do you think that?"

She hadn't told many people about Alan, only Celeste and Jenny. Not even her aunt. Still, she wanted Dawson to understand why she sometimes pulled away, why she didn't always believe the desire in his eyes, or the want-to-kiss-you-look that came over his face.

"The night of the prom, I learned that men…some men," she amended, "want sex from a woman and don't care how they get it."

"Mikala," Dawson said, shaking his head. "He was a teenage thug."

"I know. Part of me knew it even then. But what happened that night still set the stage for how I looked at myself and how I thought men looked at me. You rescued me and I knew you weren't like Carson. But that was different because we were friends."

"Maybe more if I hadn't moved away," Dawson reminded her.

"Maybe. But you *did* move away and I went to college."

"And you met someone."

"Someone who I thought I loved, and who loved me back, suddenly decided to go on the road with a band instead of earning his degree. But the reason he wanted to go on the road with that band was because he was in love with the lead singer—a very *sexy* lead singer."

Dawson was quiet for a few moments but then said, "I'm sorry you felt deserted again. But don't you realize his desertion had more to do with him than you?"

She felt a smile tease her lips. "*I'm* the counselor, remember?"

"Yes, you are." Then Dawson was right there in front of her, wrapping his arms around her, pulling her against him. "You're a beautiful, intelligent, fascinating woman who doesn't understand her own worth. You're also a very sexy woman." He ran his hands down her back, over her waist, down her hips. She could feel his arousal and she knew hers was matching it.

"You're sexy whether you realize it or not," he went on. "Whether you want to be or not. When I kiss you, your passion breaks free. Most of the time you hide it, but it's there, Mikala. I can feel it and see it and taste it."

She trembled under his hands...under his words. She did want him, almost desperately. Yet she didn't want to be in an affair that failed. She didn't want to come between him and his son. She didn't want to be a stopgap measure for Dawson while he pulled his life back together.

Taking another very deep breath, she pushed away and slowly shook her head.

But Dawson wasn't letting her turn him down that easily. "It's the gift, isn't it? It reminded you that your mother left and you think everybody else will, too. Can't you look at that gift and just think your mother remembered you?"

"She remembered me from a distance."

"You keep people at a distance, Mikala—except for Aunt Anna, Celeste and Jenny. Do you let anyone else get close?"

"I have to have a balance. I have to keep perspective, especially with my clients."

"I'm talking about your personal life. You're so busy trying to avoid getting hurt that you don't take a chance."

"What do you want me to take a chance on, Dawson? Do you know for sure you're going to stay in Miners Bluff? Isn't all of your attention focused on Luke? A chance is one thing, a monumental risk is another."

Dawson studied her for several very long moments. "The outfit looks good, no matter what you think. Maybe your mother knows you better than you believe. Maybe she has regrets about the distance between the two of you."

He started for the door then stopped. "I respect your feelings, Mikala, but you can't let your life be run by fear."

As Dawson left her office, Mikala sank into a chair, unbuckled the sandals and felt like crying.

Mikala was seated at her desk in the elementary school a few days later on her lunch break when the phone on her desk rang.

"Yes," she answered brightly, expecting to hear one of the teachers she worked with.

"Mikala?"

It wasn't one of the teachers. It was the principal. "Phil! Hi."

"Mikala, I have a situation here and I'm not sure what to do about it."

"A situation?" Maybe it was regarding one of her students.

"I have Luke Barrett in my office. He was just in a fight in the schoolyard. I have his father's numbers but I can't reach him. Luke tells me he had a business meeting. I have your name and number as the person to call if I couldn't reach him."

She remembered Dawson asking her permission to do that and she'd agreed. "I see. Is Luke hurt?"

"Well, yes, that's why I buzzed you. The nurse has examined him and I think he's just going to have a shiner. He needs to keep ice on it. I imagine his father might want to have him checked out at the urgent care center. We'll have to notify him that Luke will have a day of in-school suspension."

"I'll be right down." She and Luke were stirring things up in therapy. He'd become very agitated when she'd wanted to talk to him about his drive home in the snow with his dad, when she'd wanted him to think about everything he'd remembered the day they'd gone tubing. So what had happened today? Was Luke acting out? Or was something else going on?

When she reached the principal's office, the secretary motioned her inside. "He's waiting for you."

The door was slightly ajar and Mikala peeked in. Luke was sitting morosely in a captain's chair against the wall. Phil was at his desk, saw her and motioned her in.

Luke looked as if he'd gotten the worst of the fight. He was definitely going to have a black eye and there was a big, bright red brush burn along one side of his jaw. He was holding an ice pack to his eye, and when he looked up at her, there was defiance in his gaze.

"Luke, do you want to tell Miss Conti what happened?"

"I was in a fight," he mumbled.

"That's all he'll say," Phil said. "The other boy isn't saying anything, either."

Mikala took the icepack from Luke's eye. The bruising was already intense.

"Oh, Luke! Does it hurt?"

"Not much," he said with a shrug, then winced as he blinked.

"Your dad's going to want you to go to the doctor."

"Dad's not even answering his phone. He doesn't care."

Mikala crouched down before Luke so she was at eye level with him. "You know better than that, don't you?"

Luke stared down at his sneakers.

"Luke."

He raised his gaze to hers. "He's going to be mad I got into trouble again. Maybe *you* could take me to the doctor. Then we wouldn't have to tell him."

Kids had a great way of ignoring the obvious. "What would you tell your dad about your face and your hand?" She motioned to the scrapes there, too.

"I could just tell him I fell."

"Do you really want to lie to him?"

"No, but—"

"Besides that, Mr. Talbott will be notifying him of your suspension."

Luke's face fell even further if that was possible.

"Let me try to reach your dad again."

* * *

An hour and a half later Mikala followed Dawson and Luke up to their suite at the Purple Pansy. Father and son weren't talking…yet. Dawson had finally gotten the voice mail message and had called Mikala while she and Luke were on their way to the urgent care center. He'd met them there. Luke had been examined and checked out, but he'd remained stonily silent. Apparently Dawson had decided waiting for privacy was the better option than trying to convince Luke to talk. He'd asked her to come upstairs with them since she'd been involved in all this. She didn't know if it was a good idea or not, but she wanted to help if she could. Both Dawson and Luke had come to mean so much to her. She hated to see them floundering like this.

Inside the suite, Dawson motioned Luke to the sofa. Luke sat, looking like a shaken-up kid. All Mikala wanted to do was put her arms around him.

Dawson pushed the ottoman near Luke and sat on it, while Mikala took the chair beside the sofa. Dawson looked directly into Luke's eyes. "Now, tell me what happened."

"I got into a fight."

"I know that. Who did you fight with?"

"She already told you." He stole a glance at Mikala.

"I want *you* to tell me," Dawson repeated firmly. "Who did you fight with?"

"Brandon Sennett."

"He's in your class?"

"Yeah."

"Are you friends?"

"No. If we were friends, we wouldn't fight." That

was so obvious to Luke, and he believed it should be evident to his father, too.

"So who threw the first punch?"

"You're going to talk to Mr. Talbott anyway. He'll tell you."

"I told you, I want *you* to tell me."

"I punched him first," Luke said.

At that, Dawson paused and Mikala guessed he was figuring out where to go from there. Finally he prompted, "So tell me why."

"It wasn't anything important," Luke muttered.

"It was important enough for you to fight about. What did Brandon say?"

"He said I'm *homeless.*" When Luke looked at his dad, there was nothing but sadness there, and Mikala's heart broke for him.

She glimpsed emotion on Dawson's face just for a second. Then he hid it. She knew what he was thinking—Luke wasn't only homeless but motherless, too. His son had traumatic memory loss and all of it made Dawson feel powerless. Obvious frustration that he couldn't help his son through this difficult time made the nerve in his jaw work.

She watched as he swallowed before he spoke. "First of all, home doesn't have to be a physical place, not when you're with people who care about you. And technically, I guess we *are* homeless. But we won't be for long. I have a house to look at tomorrow."

"Here? In Miners Bluff?"

"Yes."

"I want to go back to Phoenix. I want to go back to Granddad. I didn't want him to go back there without *us!*"

"I know you miss Granddad. But I thought you were beginning to like it here."

Luke jumped up from the sofa. "I don't like it anywhere. I want to be with Granddad. I want everything the way it was before Mom died!" He ran to his room and slammed the door.

Mikala felt Dawson's regret, confusion and turmoil.

"Maybe I should have let you talk to him." Dawson stood, shaking his head then pacing. "Or maybe I should just move us back to Phoenix."

She went to Dawson and gently touched his arm. Their physical awareness of each other was instantaneous. He went still and so did she.

After a moment he asked, "It's really hard not to let a child run your world, isn't it?"

"Sometimes it's hard to remember who's in charge," she admitted.

"I know returning to Phoenix isn't the answer. I just don't know how to help Luke move forward. I talked to Dad about moving here. I've been studying personnel files. I have two foremen I can promote who would be capable. But nothing's certain yet and that's a problem for another day. Right now, I just want Luke to know he belongs here, that we can make a life here, make it better than the one we had in Phoenix for the past two years."

Mikala was impressed with Dawson's resolute attitude. She'd always admired that about him. "You'll figure this out," she said. "You and Luke will figure it out together."

He was wearing a flannel shirt today and jeans, work boots made for touring a construction site. His brown-blond hair fell over his brow and there was desire in his eyes that made heat start pooling in every feminine place.

His arm curled around her waist and he brought her close. "Your support means a lot to me and to Luke."

When he tipped her chin up, she welcomed his kiss. It was deep and thorough and it didn't last very long. She knew why. Luke was his main priority and had to be. She respected that about him and she knew she wouldn't feel so deeply about him if he didn't want the very best for his son.

Feel deeply? As she gazed into Dawson's eyes, she knew she couldn't use that euphemism any longer. She *loved* Dawson Barrett. That realization made her absolutely dizzy.

The real-estate agent opened the door to the house and led Dawson and Luke inside. Dawson had encouraged Luke to come with him. Maybe what they needed most was to make a decision *together*.

The house was empty and their footsteps echoed as Dawson led Luke over the hardwood floors into the bright kitchen, large living room and to the first-floor treasure in the back—a sunroom.

Dawson had a good feeling about the place. Despite its emptiness, it had warmth. Maybe it was the tall windows that let in lots of sun. Maybe a happy family had lived here before. He didn't know. This just felt *right*.

But Luke was quiet, not communicating, and Dawson could never tell what his son was thinking.

The real-estate agent remained downstairs as they went upstairs, realizing they could have a discussion much easier without her. She'd already pointed out all the merits.

The master suite was just right. As they viewed the other two bedrooms, Luke seemed more interested in one of them than the other. A long window seat had lids with hinges. Luke crossed to one and lifted it. "Pretty cool," he muttered.

"We could easily toss some cushions on those and you could study the constellations at night."

Luke glanced at his dad, then out the window again. "Or crawl out onto the porch roof and do it."

Dawson was horrified by that idea and Luke easily read his expression. A sly smile spread over his lips. "Just kidding, Dad."

Luke still sported a black eye that was now turning yellow and green as it healed. But the fact that he was smiling a little gave Dawson hope. "So what do you think?"

Luke shrugged. "It's got a giant backyard."

They'd been able to tell that from the view out the sliding glass doors in the dining area. "You could kick around a soccer ball, play catch...whatever you want. We could probably even cross-country ski back there. It's not too far from Clay's place, either." Was he giving it too much of a hard sell?

But Luke seemed to mull over everything he said. "Can we put a backboard on the garage?"

All at once Dawson felt relieved. If Luke could envision that, maybe he could see himself living here.

"Sure, we can. The driveway's a little steep but not right in front of the garage. It's perfect for one-on-one."

After another glance at the window seats, Luke went into the hall and peeked into the other bedroom again.

Dawson stayed put.

When Luke returned, he said, "This isn't as big as our other house."

"Does that matter?" Dawson really wanted to know what his son thought about that.

With a shrug Luke said, "Guess not." He wandered over to the window seat again and lifted the lid. Then he faced his dad. "Can I have this room?"

"If it's the one you like."

"Can I paint it whatever color I want?"

"Anything but black," Dawson said tongue-in-cheek.

But Luke's brows just arched. "Do *you* like it?"

If he seemed too enthusiastic about the place, would Luke retreat just to be contrary? Dawson didn't know. He only knew he had to be honest with his son.

"I like it. I think we can be happy here."

After Luke thought about that, he asked practically, "So when can we move in?"

Mikala glanced at Dawson as he drove toward Moonshadow Mountain early Friday afternoon. He'd called her last night and said, "Luke and I found a house." He'd sounded as if it had been the greatest achievement of his life.

"Wonderful!"

"Luke seems to like it. We signed the papers last night. How would you like to go with me to see it? We could have lunch afterward. Do you have time free tomorrow?"

Dawson knew she usually took Friday afternoon to catch up and run errands.

"After one. I guess you're sure about this one? What's it like?"

"How about if I just surprise you?"

So now she was waiting to be surprised!

The scenery changed from the town's cultivated sidewalks, maples and sycamores, to brush and pines. Celeste and Clay lived up this way in the foothills below Moonshadow Mountain. There were single-family dwellings, but also a few rural developments.

She glanced over at Dawson once or twice and saw the eagerness on his face as he drove toward their destination. It was a sunny day today and snow sloshed under their tires as it melted. When Dawson barreled through a puddle, water sprayed along the side of his SUV. Soon he pulled into a long driveway that led to a two-story home nestling into pine and aspen. It looked as if it was comfortable there. There were holly trees on either side of the house and smaller shrubs under the windows. The slate-blue siding and navy shutters coordinated well with the gray roof. Native gray stone surrounded the door and a copper roof stretched out over the porch.

"It's about ten years old," Dawson said as they mounted the steps and he inserted the key in the lock.

Moments later they were stepping over the threshold. As soon as they walked into the foyer, Mikala saw the smile on Dawson's face and knew why. There was warmth to this house with its hardwood floors and lots of wood trim. There was a stairway that led upstairs to a landing. To the left was a dining room, painted in soft green. The family room was to the right and had nubby tan, brown and rust tweed carpeting as well as a floor-to-ceiling stone fireplace. Plenty of sunlight flowed through the tall front windows.

"An independent builder built this one," Dawson explained. "He was the man I met with the day Luke was in the fight. There was a contract on this house when I first started looking, but it fell through." Dawson ran his hand over the banister, a golden oak with a glossy finish. "I'd like to have this builder on my team. The whole house is quality."

As they walked in a circle, Mikala found a sunny, yellow kitchen. There were oak cupboards there and a beautiful rust and beige ceramic tile floor. The appliances weren't old, but not brand-new, either, and the house looked as if it were ready for someone to move in. They took a tour of the upstairs and Mikala liked that as much as everything else.

"Luke wants to paint his room blue. He likes the window seats in here."

"This really seems perfect for you. I'm so glad Luke wants to make it his."

"Come on, I want to show you something."

Returning to the downstairs, Dawson guided her through the family room. There was a hall that led to the inside garage door. They passed the laundry room and went to a second door. Dawson opened it and motioned to her to precede him.

She stepped into the sunroom and couldn't help but smile. Sun poured in from three sides and the skylight above. There was a thick scatter rug on the rustic plank flooring along with a picnic basket, a few throw pillows and a bottle of wine in a cooler.

Dawson said, "Luke and I had a pizza to seal the deal last night. But I wanted to celebrate again and decided the person I wanted to celebrate with was *you*." He motioned to the bird feeders in the backyard, the pine trees at the end of the property, the sun glinting off the snow all around them. "A picnic lunch here seemed the best way to do it."

This certainly was cozier than a restaurant. Dawson seemed over-the-top happy today.

"You're excited about this, aren't you?"

He gave her a crooked grin. "I guess it shows."

"Are you happier about finding a house or about you and Luke making the decision together?"

"He talked to me more last night than he has in a long time. We called Dad together to tell him. It was the best time we've had together since…since before the accident."

Mikala knew that accident was still standing between Dawson and Luke. But it sounded as if last night had been a good start.

Dawson approached Mikala and the look in his eyes made her heart thump madly.

"Thank you. You're giving me back my son."

When Dawson reached out and the pad of his thumb brushed her cheek, she felt shaky and giddy. In a corner of her heart, a secret longing tugged at her. She could dream about moving in here with Dawson and Luke. She wasn't only in love with him but, in another startling, take-her-breath-away insight, she realized she wanted forever with him. This was the real thing. So much for warning herself to be careful. So much for keeping her distance.

So much for guarding her heart.

Chapter Nine

The fairy tale dream seemed to overwhelm Mikala as Dawson came toward her and golden light glittered all around them. They forgot about the picnic basket and the bottle of wine on the floor. Whatever she felt when she was alone with Dawson seemed to overshadow everything else! She didn't need wine to feel the heady intoxication of desiring him…needing him.

Apparently he felt the same way because as he wrapped his arms around her, he groaned. Then he kissed her before she had time to take another breath.

At the touch of his lips, she let go of who she was and imagined who she could be with Dawson. The sunshine danced around them, its glint on the snow making everything sparkle. That sparkle danced inside of her, too. When he kissed her, their desire went deeper, wetter, wilder. She'd dreamed of a moment like this with him, all happiness and sunshine and a song that played in her heart…had played in her heart since high school. It was a song with depth and feeling and magic. Her heart embraced it and her soul felt its truth. This was love. Whether she wanted it or not, it had come to her and for once in her life, she wasn't going to let fear of being hurt turn it away.

They were so hungry for each other. Dawson's hand splayed in her hair as he angled her head and ravished her mouth. His need was even more arousing than hers. Is this what it felt like to be truly desired?

She reached for his sweater, burrowed her hands beneath it and felt his torso, lean and muscled. Her fingertips touching his skin sent a shudder through him, and he acknowledged it by pulling her down on the rug and covering her body with his. That was the beginning of falling into a primal rhythm she couldn't begin to deny. Obviously, he couldn't, either.

At ease with him because this was Dawson and she was in love with him, she hurried to undo his belt as he lifted her sweater over her head. She didn't even have time to be self-conscious as he unclasped her bra and she unzipped his fly. They discarded their clothes with quick frenzied movement that had nothing to do with thought and everything to do with pleasure. As he palmed her breast, she reached for him and caressed him. Their kisses broke only for their sighs and their moans. His fingers were knowing and skilled. Hers were full of the love she felt for him.

When Dawson entered her, the pleasure was so rich she was overwhelmed by it. She twined her legs around him and took him even deeper. They made music she'd never heard before. Each verse held meaning and passion and soul-stirring words only her heart could understand. The refrain was his name and hers as they murmured to each other and blended the sound. Her climax came so fast and furious that all she could do was hold on to Dawson and tremble through it. His release came soon after as he plunged deep and she felt as if she'd always belonged to him and would belong to him forever.

They clung to each other, breathing hard, not wanting to come down to earth, yet knowing the landing was inevitable. As her breathing slowed, and their bodies cooled, she loosened her hands from around Dawson's back.

He rolled away and lay beside her. "That was incredible," he muttered. "*You* were incredible."

He was staring at her as if she really was! She reached out to take his hand. "You were, too."

Then suddenly they were both thinking the same thought, as common sense replaced passion, and logic replaced reckless impulse.

The almost harsh clarity in Dawson's eyes preceded his words. "I can't believe we didn't use protection."

A shiver of fear skipped up her back. It wasn't fear that she'd become pregnant. It was fear that she'd fallen in love and Dawson didn't feel the same.

"We weren't thinking," she said simply, as if that were some kind of an excuse for two adults who knew better.

"No, we weren't," he said on a sigh.

She didn't want to feel the gate closing between them. She didn't want to feel the distance he was going to put there. After all, hadn't he been down a similar road before?

Touching his forearm, she asked, "What are the

chances? The odds are on our side I *won't* get pregnant."

"It's Russian roulette, Mikala. This isn't about odds, not unless you're on the pill."

"I'm not. I don't have any reason to be."

Dawson looked away from her, as if he was trying to figure out something...maybe what he would do if she *was* pregnant.

His gaze was troubled as he brought it back to hers. "My life is a mess. And until Luke is doing better, I can't consider a relationship, not a serious one. But I want to be with you, Mikala. I don't want to close the door between us. Is that possible?"

Was that possible? Could she accept being Dawson's— what? Friend? Could they go back to that?

As if he'd read her thoughts, he was shaking his head. "I don't know what comes next. Maybe we can all just be together more. Can we try that?"

She thought about Luke and what was best for him, too. He was beginning to trust her. His relationship with Dawson had taken a step forward. Better not to disrupt that right now.

She wanted to ask the question that was uppermost in her mind. *What happens if I get pregnant?* But she didn't. That was just too big and serious to consider. And just as serious was the fact that she couldn't walk away from Dawson. That simply wasn't an option. She wanted to spend more time with him and with Luke, too...outside of their sessions. Although she hadn't expected any of this to happen, although she now had a new worry, she could still hear the faint music deep in her heart that had begun when she and Dawson had made love. She couldn't say no to Dawson. She simply couldn't.

"I'd like to spend more time with you...and with Luke." She'd like to help him build a new life. But she would look into finding Luke a new therapist.

That would be the best solution for them all.

On Sunday afternoon, Mikala glanced around Luke's room. They'd painted early that morning and the paint was already dry, ready for the next step. The room was coming together. But she and Dawson weren't. They couldn't. Not with Luke around. They didn't want to give him something else he had to deal with. So they kept their distance as they painted and worked to make every room in the house perfect.

Luke seemed to like the steel-blue color he'd chosen for his room. Mikala was moving one of the tarps where they'd be painting a graphite square so that Luke could write on it, when she felt Dawson enter the room. She didn't turn around.

After he came up behind her, his hand was light on her shoulder. Still, she could feel the searing heat. And when she straightened, he was right there. They were nose to nose and, if she wanted, she could rest her head on his chest.

Where had *that* thought come from?

She swallowed hard. "What's Luke up to?"

"He's opening the boxes in the garage and pulling out his speakers. He wants to set those up almost before anything else," Dawson explained with a wry grin. "So I thought I'd just slip in here and..." His hand slid behind her neck then he bent his head and kissed her. It was a hungry kiss, filled with wanting to be together again. But she didn't know if that was all he wanted. Nevertheless she responded as she always did. Every womanly sensation came alive. She gave and took as much as he did, wildly taking advantage of the free moment, wondering what it would be like to have many free moments with Dawson.

Stop dreaming, she warned herself as she pulled away from him. *Dreams don't come true.*

In the flash between wanting forever and accepting now, she remembered the dream she'd had of her mother coming home, of taking Mikala in her arms, of saying she was going to stay. Dreams of Alan telling her they'd make beautiful music together played like an old recording, put away yet never forgotten. She remembered wondering after prom night, whether Dawson would call. She'd pictured them holding hands as they walked to class. But then he'd moved away.

Dawson pushed her hair away from her face with both of his hands and asked, "What are you thinking?"

Flustered, she knew she couldn't tell him. She would not make herself that vulnerable. Protecting her heart had become second nature. Yes, Dawson's kisses were one of the keys to unlocking it…and making love with him had thrown wide the door. But she'd closed it again because she knew his feelings didn't match hers. She could only be vulnerable if he was just as vulnerable and that wasn't in Dawson's nature, either.

"That this house is going to be perfect for you and Luke."

He looked as if he didn't believe her. Yet he also didn't push, maybe because he didn't want to know too much.

They heard Luke clomping up the stairs and moved

apart. Was hiding their attraction from Luke the best strategy for any of them? She remembered what her aunt had said. *Luke is a smart boy.*

But keeping their connection—she couldn't think of it as an affair—from him seemed to be the safest route, and right now that's the one they were taking.

As Luke came into the room, his arms full of equipment, Dawson hurried to help him.

"Do you want to paint the graphite square?" Mikala asked. "Or do you want me to do it while you set up your equipment?"

Luke grinned at her. "Will you? I want this ready for when my other stuff comes tomorrow."

"No problem," Mikala told him, reaching for the can of graphite paint.

By the time Mikala finished with the bulletin-board-size square, Dawson had hammered brackets into the wall for shelves and was positioning them. Luke was sorting through his books.

Mikala glanced out the window. "It's snowing again."

Luke stared out the window at the view and then got up and walked over to it.

She propped her brush in a bucket of water. Her gaze found Dawson's. He went to the window beside his son and capped his shoulder. "What's on your mind?"

Silent for a long time, Luke finally said, "I think it was snowing the night of Mom's accident."

Dawson glanced at Mikala briefly, but his attention switched back to his son. "Do you remember watching it fall?"

Luke shook his head. "Not really. It's just—a feeling."

Mikala didn't want to crowd him. She also didn't want to intrude on real communication between Dawson and Luke. But she was here, and she wanted to help.

Crossing to the other side of the ten-year-old, she stared out the window at the snow-frosted pines and aspen. "Maybe if you let yourself feel, memories might come along with those emotions."

As if he was trying with all his might to remember, Luke shut his eyes. But when he opened them, he looked disappointed and confused. "What if I *never* remember what happened?"

Dawson stepped in before she could. "If you remember, we'll deal with what you remember. If you don't, we're going to start a new life here and be happy doing it. I want you to know you're not alone, Luke. I'm always going to be here. Granddad is just a phone call away. Mikala's here, too."

"And Aunt Anna," Luke said as if they might forget about her.

Mikala's throat tightened with emotion because Luke was starting to realize he *did* have people who cared about him. Maybe feeling secure and comfortable and loved would help him allow memories to surface. She fervently hoped so.

Dawson said, "Speaking of Aunt Anna. I told her we'd give her a break tonight. How about pizza?"

"Can we get buffalo wings, too?" Luke asked.

"Sure."

"Can I call in the order?"

"You bet. The phone book's on the counter downstairs."

"I'll go get it. Are you coming down?"

"As soon as Mikala and I clean up a bit."

Luke looked around his bedroom at the shelves on the freshly painted walls, his stereo system sitting on the floor just waiting for the stand.

He said to Mikala, "Thanks for helping set up my room."

"You're welcome."

As Luke galloped down the steps, she and Dawson migrated toward each other.

"Was that another breakthrough?" he asked.

"The feelings are part of remembering. I'll explore them more with him when we have our session this week. It will have to be Thursday, though. I have a conference over the weekend."

Dawson looked surprised. "Where?"

"In Santa Fe. I'll be leaving Friday and coming back Monday."

"Do you have much preparation to do?"

"My workshop presentation is almost finished. I'll be adding the final touches to it tonight."

"Luke isn't the only one grateful for you helping here today. I know your life's busy."

"I like spending time with you and Luke. I wouldn't be here if I didn't."

"Maybe after you get back, we'll have some time alone again."

Was he asking her if she wanted that? Or was he assuming that she did?

His heated gaze was filled with the visions she had in the middle of the night of the two of them making love. But she was afraid making love with him again would reveal the vulnerability she'd been keeping hidden. A few days away in Santa Fe might be a good thing. A few days away could give her perspective. A few days away might give her the answers she couldn't seem to find here.

Mikala debated with herself about calling Dawson from her hotel room in Santa Fe the following Saturday night. She'd returned to her room to shower and change for dinner with a colleague. Finished dressing early, she thought about Dawson…about making love with him…about whether or not her period would be on time. Even though she'd been busy since she'd arrived at the conference, she couldn't help thinking about Dawson and Luke. Her session with Luke on Thursday had been productive. He'd talked about his furniture arriving at the house and looking forward to really moving on. When she'd probed about his feeling that snow had fallen the day of the accident, he couldn't remember anything else. She knew, however, once the floodgates started to open, memories could pour out. She didn't want Luke and Dawson to have to handle that on their own.

Without hesitating longer, she found Dawson in her contact list and called his cell phone. He picked up after the first ring.

"Hi," he said as if he was glad to hear from her.

"Hi, yourself. Is this a bad time?"

"Not at all. Luke and I were shifting some of our new furniture around. It hasn't all been delivered yet but we're going to spend the night here anyway."

Spend the night. The phrase brought visions into her

head of what she and Dawson had done, of what they could do in a bed. She tried to steer her mind away from that track.

"Aunt Anna is going to miss you at the Purple Pansy."

"Are you really thinking about your Aunt Anna?" Dawson asked, his voice a bit husky.

She decided to be honest with him. "No. I was thinking about you and me in the sunroom."

He didn't respond right away as if he was surprised by her honesty. "I was thinking about the same thing. I was thinking about my new king-size bed and how it would be a lot more comfortable than the sunroom floor."

"Dawson—"

"Luke went up to his room. He's checking my laptop to look for a poster he wants for his wall. So I'm free to talk."

"And what would you like to say?" She found herself a bit breathless and realized just the tone of his voice could do that.

"Well, for starters, tell me what you're wearing."

She wasn't sure where this was leading, but she decided to follow. "I'm wearing a cocktail dress."

"What color?"

"It's blue."

"Short or long?"

"Above the knee. It has long sleeves and a V-neck." If he wanted to play this game, she could too.

"Zipper down the back?" he asked.

"Yes."

"Okay, then I want you to imagine something. Imagine me unzipping that zipper. Imagine me brushing the dress from your shoulders and kissing the nape of your neck."

Oh, she could imagine it all right. She could imagine it all too well. "And then?" she asked with her voice catching. "Then I get to unbutton your shirt? And run my hands over your chest?"

His silence made her wonder if maybe Luke had come downstairs. Finally he admitted, "I started this. I just didn't realize how...exciting it could get."

"You want me to rebutton your shirt?" she teased.

He laughed. "No. But maybe we should save this conversation for midnight when I know we won't be interrupted. Do you have a workshop tomorrow morning?"

"I have breakfast at eight."

"They do keep you busy."

"Yes, they do."

"How did your presentation go?"

"It went well. I had a lot of positive comments afterward."

"As well you should. You're good, Mikala. You're skilled at what you do."

"Sometimes skill isn't enough. How's Luke? Has he remembered anything else?"

"Not that I can tell. We put up a basketball net and shot hoops in the snow. Tomorrow Celeste invited him to go along with her and Abby to the movies. He seemed to like the idea. So Noah, Riley, Clay and I are going to play poker while they're out."

"That will be good for Luke. And you."

There was a knock on Mikala's door. She checked her watch. Ben was early. "Dawson, can you hold on a minute? Someone's at my door."

She went to the door, opened it and smiled at Ben Cromwell. He was a professor at USC and they'd given workshops together in the past. "Hi, Ben. Come on in. I won't be long."

"Ben?" Dawson asked. "Do you have a dinner date?"

"Not exactly."

"What does that mean?" The warmth had left his voice and he sounded...jealous? Was that possible?

She quickly explained, "Ben teaches music theory at USC. We're often on panels together at these conferences. We're on a panel together tomorrow morning so we decided to have dinner to prepare notes."

"I see," Dawson said, but she wasn't sure he did see. "Have you known him long?" he asked and his tone sounded casual again.

"About five years. After dinner there's a cocktail party and we'll be going to that. It's all part of the conference."

"Well, I won't keep you from dinner," he, said. "Enjoy yourself. We'll save that midnight conversation for another time."

She was disappointed they weren't going to have that midnight conversation, but she knew she had to be fresh in the morning. Yet she didn't want their call to end like this...abruptly...with maybe a misunderstanding on his part.

"Dawson, I called because I'm not so busy that I'm not thinking about you and Luke. I just wanted you to know that."

His silence told her he hadn't expected that. Finally he responded with a gruff, "Thanks for calling, Mikala. I'll talk to you when you get back. I hope the rest of the conference is successful."

"Bye, Dawson."

When she closed her phone, she felt unsettled, as if she'd given too much away...as if she'd done the wrong thing by calling.

When she saw Dawson in person again, she'd know.

Chapter Ten

The following afternoon Dawson sat in Clay's kitchen with Clay, Noah and Riley, playing poker.

"So Zack's in DC?" Riley asked Dawson, as Clay dealt the first hand and Noah filled the potato chip bowl.

"He's working on a documentary about veterans," Dawson explained, taking a handful of pretzels and setting them on his plate. "He's making a couple of stops on his way back here. I think he'll be gone about two weeks."

"That's got to be tough for him and Jenny. Newly-weds don't like to be apart," Clay commented. Clay had only been married five months himself, so he knew.

Celeste came into the kitchen and grabbed her car keys from a dish on the counter. "Help yourselves to the pizza pockets whenever you feel like it. The fridge is stocked. The kids and I are leaving for the movies now. Remember there's chocolate cake on the counter."

"Beautiful and can cook, too," Noah said as he shook his head. "You don't know how lucky you are."

"Oh, yes, I do," Clay protested, pulled his wife toward him for a quick kiss and then let her go. "See you in a while."

"In a while," she agreed with a coy smile and then left the kitchen.

Watching them, Dawson realized he and Kelly had never had that kind of marriage. He wasn't exactly sure what that kind of marriage was. There was a quiet but deep intimacy between Clay and Celeste that he'd never experienced with Kelly. It was the same kind of silent communication he'd noticed between Jenny and Zack. Just how did a couple reach that level? He'd married Kelly because that had been the right thing to do. But had the "right" thing been wrong?

Each of the men bet their hands.

"Have you heard from Brenna since the reunion?" Noah asked Riley.

Seated next to Riley, Dawson saw the man's shoulders tense, his spine stiffen.

"Why do you think I would?" Riley asked Noah, moving a stack of poker chips from one side of his plate to the other.

"You left the reunion together," Noah said amiably, curiosity in his gaze.

"We just fell into conversation at the reunion. But the rift between our families makes it hard to be... friends."

Dawson noticed Riley was definitely uncomfortable with the whole conversation. Sure enough, Riley pushed back his chair and snagged a pizza pocket. Glancing at Dawson, he remarked, "How are things with you and Mikala? Are you officially dating?"

"No," Dawson said very quickly. Too quickly. No. Not dating. But they'd made love and he felt a bond with her. After examining his reaction to her phone call, he'd had to admit he'd been jealous she was having dinner with a colleague.

But they *weren't* dating.

"She's helping Luke. When we were staying at the Purple Pansy, she and I ran into each other a lot." At the raised brows from the other men, he added, "My life is too complicated to even consider anything serious. And Mikala... She's got her own issues, just as we all do."

"Issues? What issues?" Noah asked. "*I'm* an open book."

They all knew that wasn't true. Noah's job meant he had a very public persona but he also had a very private life. He'd worked in the Phoenix Police Department before taking the job as chief in Miners Bluff. No one knew exactly what had happened in Phoenix, but something had, something that had changed him.

"It doesn't matter if we have issues," Clay protested. "What matters is that we share them with the person we care about. I just think it's a lot harder for guys than it is for women."

"Sometimes it's not so easy for *them,* either." Dawson remembered the expression on Mikala's face after she'd gotten an email from her mother, after she'd received the package in the mail. Maybe when two people could talk about history that hurt...maybe when

KAREN ROSE SMITH 169

that became easy, that's how a man knew he'd found the right woman.

The right woman to have an affair with? The right woman to live with? The right woman to love?

Dawson took three cards from his hand and pushed them over to Riley. "Three new ones." If he was lucky, he'd end up with two pair.

If he was lucky, Mikala's dinner with her colleague had meant absolutely nothing.

He was getting in deeper than he wanted to admit.

Mikala wasn't ignoring Dawson…she wasn't. Returning from the conference, she'd had to catch up with appointments as well as helping Anna with the B and B. That's all it was. She was busy.

Besides, Dawson wasn't under the same roof any more. Things were different now. They didn't run into each other. She hadn't called him again. Wasn't that best? She was having trouble finding another music therapist to recommend to Dawson for Luke.

When the doorbell in her studio rang, she knew who it was. She had a session with Luke and, of course, Dawson would be bringing him.

Dawson didn't come into her office with his son. His gaze held hers as he said, "I'll be back around five, right?"

"That should do it," she agreed, looking toward Luke who'd already gone into the music room.

The silence went a beat too long. Filling it, maybe not wanting to see Dawson leave just yet, she asked, "Are you enjoying the new house?"

"It's coming along."

Again awkward silence settled between them.

Dawson broke it this time. "Luke mentioned he'd like to see Aunt Anna. Is it okay if we go over to visit after his appointment?"

"Sure. She'd like that. She misses you."

His gaze seemed to inquire if *she* did too, but he didn't ask the question. "Okay then, I'll see you at five."

Mikala shut the door against the March chill and went to the music room. Luke handed her his iPod as soon as she sat in one of the chairs. She'd asked him if she could see his music list. She scrolled through it. "Very diverse taste. Only one kind is missing."

"What?" Luke asked.

"Country. You don't like country?"

"No," he said adamantly. "I don't."

"No Jason Aldean, Carrie Underwood, Brad Paisley?"

"No," he said again, even more adamantly. "I don't."

"Would you like to tell me why?"

"The same reason Dad doesn't like some of the singers I like."

Something about Luke's answer didn't ring true. So she went down a different road. "I'd like to try something a little different today."

"Like what?" Luke asked warily.

"I'd like to put your iPod on a dock, hook it up to the speakers, and while it plays, I'd like you to draw for me."

"Draw what?"

"Nothing in particular. Whatever comes into your mind. Do you think you could try that?"

"I don't draw very good."

"I don't care what it looks like. It can even be abstract. It's sort of like when you're playing the piano and you don't have music in front of you. I'd like you to do the same thing with crayons—just let the music play and you draw."

Luke shrugged. "Sounds okay to me."

She guessed what he was thinking. Anything was better than her asking questions and him having to answer them. But freedom for him to draw whatever he wanted might give her a clue as to what he was thinking, might let a few of his memories pop out.

After she hooked up his iPod, he sat at a table and chair with a sheet of drawing paper, colored pencils and crayons all around it. They'd set his device on shuffle and, at first, Luke seemed awkward with the whole process. But then he picked up a crayon and just started scribbling. One song segued into another. His colors and lines and shapes spread from one piece of paper to the next. Finally instead of random pictures of trees or cactus or cars or dogs, a new picture slowly emerged. Mikala just watched, studying Luke's body language, expressions passing over his face. Where at the beginning, the process had been almost a lark, now there was intensity about him. Mikala didn't peek over his shoulder, just gave him space. But she suspected something emotional was emerging, something other than a simple drawing that might mean nothing.

When he'd finished, he sat back, put down the crayon and didn't pick up another.

"I don't want to do this anymore," he said.

Mikala switched off the music and sat at the table beside him, studying the pictures one by one. She commented on each, asked him a few questions, listened to his answers.

When she reached the final one, she said simply, "Can you tell me about this one?"

"That's me and my mom," he said pointing to the figures.

Mikala pointed to the woman. "Your mom had red hair?"

Luke nodded, his eyes misting over.

"Just from this picture, I can tell you thought she was pretty." He'd dressed her in a pink sweater and slacks with a scarf around her neck.

"She was *really* pretty."

"Were you and your mom doing anything special in this picture?"

He just had them standing there and Mikala wanted to know what scene had come into his mind.

"It's just me and her, not doing anything."

But then on the far side of the page there was a fence and a shadowy figure standing behind it. The figure wasn't clear, but it looked like a man.

"Can you tell me about the rest of the picture?"

"No. I don't know why I drew it."

Mikala tapped her finger on the figure. "Do you know who this is?"

"No. I don't know. I guess it's Dad."

Was it Dawson on the outside looking in? Or was it someone else? Luke was getting agitated and her instincts told her pushing him now wouldn't be a good idea. She pointed to the credenza. "Why don't you pick out one of your pieces of sheet music and play it for me? I like to hear you play."

"That's cool." He seemed much more relaxed with that idea. And that's what she wanted—Luke relaxed enough that his guard might slip and let his memories through. Searching through the sheet music, he pulled out his favorite.

Mikala didn't want Luke to dread these sessions. She wanted part of him to look forward to them.

Because if he was relaxed with her, he might just remember exactly what had happened the night of the accident.

Mikala suspected Luke couldn't resist one of Aunt Anna's pies or one of her dinners. Neither could Dawson. She'd invited them to stay for supper and they'd readily agreed.

What Mikala couldn't resist was watching Dawson as he ate his slice of pie. His hands were masculine, his fingers long. She could remember every place he'd touched…every place he'd kissed. She wished they were back on easy footing again. So when Luke asked if he could play gin rummy with Anna and Dawson motioned Mikala into the hallway, she followed him.

She could see Dawson struggle with what to say. He didn't even start with a transitional opener. He just jumped in. "I shouldn't have gotten an attitude about you going to dinner with a colleague at the conference."

Relief flooded through her. The edge she'd heard in his voice hadn't been her imagination. "Why *did* you?" If Dawson could be honest with her, maybe there was hope.

"You're going to make me admit it, aren't you?" He seemed perturbed at the thought.

At that she had to smile. "Admit what?" she asked innocently.

Shaking his head, he gave her a penetrating look.

"That I was jealous. I had visions of that dinner turning into something like...we were talking about."

She said quickly, "He really was just a colleague. You have nothing to be jealous about. You know me, Dawson. I don't—"

"Yes, I do know that," he said on a blown-out breath. Then he wrapped his arms around her, brought her close, and kissed her.

Each of their kisses became a new melody. This one was sweet and tender until it turned into all passion and living-for-the-moment. Totally involved in responding to his lips nibbling hers, his tongue chasing hers, she was disappointed when he put on the brakes. But he didn't release her. He didn't let her go. Instead he held her and rocked her a little, and she delighted in the joy of holding and being held.

Finally he leaned away. "I'd better get Luke back to the house. He has a science test to study for. But—" He stopped. "I want to spend some time with *you*. Are you free tomorrow afternoon? I'd like to take you to lunch."

She liked the fact that Dawson remembered her schedule.

She also liked the idea that he wanted to be with her. "I have a session at eleven-thirty, but I'll be free by one. Do you want me to drive to your place?"

"No. I'll pick you up."

"It's a date," she responded a bit breathlessly. But he didn't disagree. So the butterflies in her stomach would settle down a bit, she focused on a subject that was on her mind. "Something came up in my session with Luke today."

Dawson looked surprised she was mentioning the session.

"How does he feel about country music?" Since Dawson kept watch over Luke's downloads, she hoped he'd know.

"Kelly had it on all the time. He always liked it. Why?"

"He didn't want to listen to it, and I wondered if that just started or if he's always liked other music better."

"Come to think of it, the last time he showed me what was on his iPod, I didn't notice any country. He must have deleted it. Any idea why?"

"No. It could be something as simple as it was playing in the car the night of the accident."

"I never thought of that," Dawson said soberly.

Suddenly they heard footsteps running into the hallway, but they didn't jump apart as they might have once done. They were standing close, arm to arm, and they stayed that way.

Luke didn't seem to notice. Grinning, he said, "I won, Dad. Aunt Anna said we could take along the rest of the pie."

Dawson laughed. "Now that's a prize we'll both enjoy." He crossed to Luke and dropped his arm around his shoulders. "Come on. Let's go home."

As Mikala watched, Luke didn't pull away. Maybe Dawson and Luke were really both healing. Maybe her dream wasn't so far-fetched after all.

When Dawson arrived at Mikala's studio on Friday afternoon, she was sliding percussion instruments into a box.

She answered the door, her heart tripping fast, her expectations for the afternoon too high. They climbed even higher when she saw him. Dressed in a hunter-green sweater and black jeans, she couldn't imagine him looking any sexier.

"Come on in," she said. "I'll just straighten up the music room and grab my coat."

Dawson looked relaxed as he entered her office. "I thought we could drive into Flagstaff and eat at Charly's at the Weatherford. That hotel has as much Western charm as Miners Bluff."

She laughed. She knew the restaurant at the Weatherford Hotel and appreciated its historic appeal. "I'd like that," she said.

In spite of looking forward to the afternoon, she couldn't help thinking about the two pregnancy tests she'd bought but hadn't used yet. Her period was late and she was never late. She knew she was burying her head in the sand, but neither she nor Dawson were ready for any life-changing news. What difference would a few more days make?

She went into the music room and lowered a set of maracas into the instrument box. Stowing it on a shelf in the closet, she shut the door.

When she turned around, Dawson was right there. Something about his expression made her feel expectant.

"I have something for you," he said.

When she gazed into his eyes, she saw his affection for her and his desire. But was there love?

"It's not my birthday," she joked.

He handed her a small white box. "Just consider this a belated Valentine's Day present."

When she opened the box with trembling fingers, she found a gold chain holding a charm keeper with a rose at the bezel. A tiny gold piano dangled from the keeper. "Oh, Dawson. This is beautiful! I don't know what to say."

"Say you'll wear it." He was grinning at her, and she felt so much joy she could hardly contain it. Her fingers shook as she plucked the necklace from the box and held it up. The sunlight shining through the windows glinted off the gold.

Sliding his long fingers under the chain, Dawson took it from her. "Let me put it on for you."

When she turned around, there was silence for a few moments. She could feel Dawson behind her, remembering how she'd known his body in intimate ways. Was he remembering, too?

He brushed her hair aside, his fingertips grazing the nape of her neck, and she shivered at his touch. He leaned toward her, his jaw near her temple.

"I think about you in my arms all the time," he said in a husky voice.

"I do, too," she admitted.

This time his fingers lingered on her neck, then stroked through her hair. He was making the quivering inside her become a longing-filled ache. She wanted him again, and from the way he was touching her, he wanted her.

His lips were smooth and hot and firm when he pushed aside the neck of her sweater and kissed her shoulder. She felt as if she were going to collapse in a swoon at his feet.

"Dawson, wait," she said breathlessly, turning toward him.

"You don't want me to put the necklace on you?" His brow was arched but there was a mischievous gleam in his eyes.

She suddenly couldn't seem to find words, but she cleared her throat and did the best she could. "I don't want us to be disturbed when you do."

It only took her a matter of seconds to go to her door, turn around the sign that said In Session and lock the dead bolt. She was back before him, feeling more wanton than she'd ever felt in her life. Is this what love did? Is this what desire did? For her, at the moment, the two were one and she couldn't figure it out.

This time he took the chain and his arms seemed to surround her as he hung it around her neck. Then he kissed her cheek.

"Turn around."

When she did, he wasn't looking at the charm. He was looking at her in a way that made her want to cry. Had any man ever looked at her like that before? She'd never felt this much love or this overwhelming need to be part of him.

He slid his fingers under the charm, touching the point between her breasts. Desire began rippling through her, weakening her knees.

"You brought music back into my life, Mikala, in more ways than one."

His kiss was hypnotically erotic. It told her what he wanted and the immediacy of his need. She held him tight, kissed him back, pressed into him, ready to fulfill his fantasies as long as they were about her.

They kissed until they both needed air. When they broke apart, took in deep breaths, they gazed into each other's eyes and then kissed again. Mikala's hands were in Dawson's hair, ruffling through it, touching the back of his neck, caressing his ear.

He pulled away and said, "You make me want too much."

Want too much physically? Or emotionally?

He didn't give her a chance to think further about it. His hands shaped her breasts into his palms and a maelstrom whirled inside of Mikala. She felt defenseless against his passion. Yet she knew she had power because when she slipped her hand under his sweater, his groan of pleasure told her it was so. His mouth was possessive, his hands greedy, every touch glazed with passion.

He was careful when he lifted off her sweater, so he didn't damage the necklace. He fingered the charm, let it sink between her breasts, then he toyed with it, creating sensations that were making her crazy.

"Dawson," she breathed almost on a whimper.

"I like the way it looks there," he said roughly with a bit of amusement.

She slid his sweater up, letting her fingers sift through his chest hair. His green eyes darkened, then he roughly lifted his sweater over his shoulders, over his head and tossed it to the floor. He removed a packet from his pocket and she knew he'd come prepared.

But he hadn't been prepared before. What were the chances she was pregnant?

Then as he removed his jeans and briefs, she lost the ability to think. She must have been standing still just watching him because he smiled at her.

Then his hands went to the waistband of her slacks. "Want some help?"

"Only yours," she said honestly.

He stopped for a moment as if there were more

meaning to her words than he wanted to hear. But then he helped her undress until she was as naked as he was.

Leading her to the sofa, he lay back and then pulled her on top of him. She felt self-conscious at first, much too exposed. What did he want her to do? But Dawson didn't seem to care what she did as long as she touched him, as long as she kissed him, as long as she held him. They were driving each other crazy with the fore-play but she realized this was what he wanted, because when they did join, their union would be explosive.

After he prepared himself, he let her take control. This was a new experience for her, a freeing experi-ence. As she straddled him, she realized maybe Daw-son had guessed it would be that way. There was a knowing in his eyes. He wanted to erase any bad ex-perience she'd ever had. He wanted to show her that being with a man meant something.

As she slowly let him fill her, her world spun. She belonged to Dawson and she wanted him to belong to her.

Wildly pleasurable sensations wiped away the thought of consequences or the future. Only the union of their bodies mattered, only the rocking motion that brought them both pleasure. She found bliss a few sec-onds before he did, then he was reaching for it, too, reaching for her, holding on to her as if he'd never let her go. Her climax was the most erotic, body-shivering moment she'd ever known.

Dawson seemed unable to catch his breath, too, and she was so happy about that. They fit together so per-fectly. But after long moments of lying there together, Mikala needed an answer.

"Dawson?" she asked.

"Hmm?"

"What are you thinking?"

She felt him tense and then he relaxed again. "I'm thinking this is better than lunch at Charly's."

She could ask more questions. She could spoil the mood. Or she could enjoy the afternoon for what it was—her time with Dawson.

However, the intensity of her feelings at this moment told her tomorrow morning, she would be using that pregnancy test. She had to know one way or the other and so did Dawson.

Maybe then they could figure out where they went from here.

Chapter Eleven

Mikala waited until her aunt had left the house for choir practice early Saturday morning. Not that Anna would ever barge in or anything, but Mikala needed privacy to do the pregnancy test, to be able to face the facts of whatever the results were.

She'd had a wonderful afternoon with Dawson yesterday. They'd gone to lunch after all and had laughed, told stories, brushed elbows and thighs under the table as if they held a wonderful secret. *She* did. She loved him. But Dawson was still just on the edge of a new life, trying to balance his future and Luke's. He'd asked her to come to dinner with them tonight. But with her period late now, she had to do this. She had to find out for sure if she was carrying Dawson's baby.

Her hand shook as she took the box into her bathroom and opened it. This test would be crystal clear.

There would be no mistaking the results. Still she'd bought two tests just to make sure.

Fifteen minutes later Mikala had finished using the second test. She stared down at the two sticks on the vanity and didn't know which emotion was going to win her heart—joy that she was pregnant with Dawson's baby...or panic about what Dawson would have to say.

She had two counseling sessions this morning and an in-home session this afternoon. And then she'd have to get ready for dinner with Dawson and Luke.

Just how was she going to tell Dawson that he was going to be a dad...again?

Mikala was nervous as she drove to Dawson's house. She might as well admit it. She just didn't want her anxiety to ruin dinner. She'd have to hide it. After Luke went to bed, then she and Dawson could talk.

But what would they talk about? A future? Or no future? Her hopes were all mixed up with her fears. The past was all mixed up with the present.

On Dawson's porch she rang the bell and waited. When he opened the door, he wasn't smiling. The first thing he said was, "Luke's upstairs. I just have a minute or two to tell you this."

"What?"

"He had a nightmare last night, a bad one, the first one in a couple of months. He said it was different. He said he couldn't remember what was in it. When he woke up, everything was gray and he didn't know what was real and what he'd dreamed. But in the midst of it, he was a mess. He was crying. He was calling for Kelly. It was awful. All I could do was hold him."

"His memories are trying to get through, Dawson. I

suggest we set up an earlier session for him than next Thursday. Maybe with me he can relax enough to let some of it out."

"Why can't he be relaxed with me?" Dawson wondered aloud.

"Because you're his father, and there might be something he doesn't want to tell you. In the meantime," she went on, "we have to show him we know how to have a good time and he can, too. It isn't one or the other, Dawson. He has to meld what happened into his real life."

The lines around Dawson's eyes eased and a slip of a smile turned up his lips. "You always bring perspective to this."

Now if she only had perspective on what she had to tell him. She could do it now...before they started the evening.

But Luke came barreling down the stairs. "Hi, Mikala. Come see my room. It looks great. Dad and I got a spread last night. It's got horses and trees and elk."

Taking a deep breath, she said enthusiastically, "I can't wait to see it." Then she followed Luke up the steps, down the hall and into his room, knowing change was brewing for all of them.

"I got some red pillows for my bed, too, to go with it, and Dad found the horse print and the one of the yellow Mustang for my wall."

"Looking very cool. What's this on your graphite wall?" He'd written: *Jake, one o'clock, Sunday.*

"Oh, it's nothing," he said. "Jake's coming here tomorrow. He's learning to play the guitar. I think I might like to do that, too."

She waited for more.

"We're just going to hang out, maybe play basket-ball."

Mikala had considered having a session with Luke tomorrow. But now she rethought the idea. If Luke had made a friend, that interaction was just as impor-tant. "Sounds like fun. I bet you'll have a great time."

Luke did seem to be settling in, did seem to be com-municating more with his dad. This could still take many, many months, but he was on the right track. Their next session might reveal something or it might reveal nothing. Just maybe, the locked box of Luke's memories was coming open and she would be there to help unravel them.

She told herself to relax through dinner. Dawson had made shrimp scampi and rice and there was a salad. They'd kidded each other about culinary skills as Luke explained he'd made the salad. But Mikala discovered the smell of the shrimp was almost turning her green. She pushed them around her plate, ate the rice and nibbled on the salad. Since Dawson had made brownies for dessert, she managed half of one of those.

"Watching your weight?" he kidded her, and she wanted to blurt out everything right then and there. But Luke was devouring a second brownie and she knew her news had to wait for a private moment.

She just responded lightly, "I'm always watching my weight," and realized putting food in her mouth was going to take on a whole new meaning with a lit-tle life growing inside of her. She put her hand to her stomach and thought about everything that was going to happen. She was *so* excited!

But would Dawson feel the same way?

The three of them cleaned up the kitchen together

and then Dawson surprised her again by producing his guitar. A fire was going strong in the fireplace. Luke pointed out the piano that fit perfectly along a side wall. Then they settled on the comfortable furniture Dawson and Luke had chosen and Dawson started with "Blowin' in the Wind." Luke didn't know the song, but as Mikala and Dawson sang, he soon joined in. Just for the heck of it, Dawson did a rendition of "Jingle Bells" that made Luke laugh. After another round of brownies for Luke and Dawson, Luke said good-night and went up to his room.

Mikala's heart began to pound and her palms felt a little sweaty. Maybe her hormones were already in an uproar. Or maybe she was just scared.

Dawson moved closer to her on the couch and put his arm around her.

To postpone the inevitable, she said, "Since Luke is having a friend over tomorrow, how about Monday after school for his next session?"

Dawson thought about it. "Monday's good." Then he brought her even closer for a kiss.

She breathed in his aftershave and drank in everything that was Dawson. She loved kissing him. She loved touching him. She loved *him*.

Because she did, she settled her hand on his roughly woven tan sweater.

He regarded her with amusement. "Afraid Luke will come down and find us?"

She inhaled deeply, trying to calm every nerve jumping around inside of her. "That's one concern," she admitted.

"You have others?" The amusement faded and he became serious.

"I do. I have something to tell you."

He looked worried now. "About Luke?"

"No, not about Luke. About me. About *us*. I'm pregnant, Dawson."

She'd seen many emotions cross Dawson's face in the past months, but she'd never seen the shock that was there now. He looked as if she'd just told him the world was going to end.

When Dawson didn't say anything, Mikala couldn't be silent, too. "Say something."

He sat forward on the sofa, raked his hand through his hair, studied her for a moment, then gazed into the fire. "How do you feel about this?"

His tone was cautious. She wanted to throw her arms around him, tell him she loved him, and that she was ecstatic about the pregnancy. But he wasn't saying the words she wanted to hear. He wasn't saying, *Together we'll make this work* or *I love you*. He was pulling away and becoming remote.

She felt her walls going up again, too. Holding on to her pride suddenly became more important than telling him how she honestly felt.

To her dismay, her voice shook a little as she said, "Your baby is a special gift. And I want to be a mom, Dawson."

He ran a hand over his face. "I need time to think about this. Luke is my priority and I have to figure out what's best for all of us."

The flames popped in the fireplace, emphasizing what he'd said. She wanted to protest and tell him, *You don't have to think about what's best for me. I know what's best for me.* But she knew his history. She knew he'd married Kelly because she'd gotten pregnant. And although Dawson loved Luke dearly, he might not be sure now that that had been the best decision he'd made.

Her silence seemed better suited to the situation right now. If she kept her mouth closed, foolish things wouldn't come tumbling out of it. More than anyone, she knew Dawson couldn't—wouldn't—choose her over Luke. More than anyone, she knew what it felt like when a parent had divided attention or paid no attention to a child at all.

"Maybe I'd better go."

When Dawson didn't protest, she couldn't help but feel like that child again who'd been abandoned and deserted and left behind. He was going to let her go. He wasn't going to tell her what he was thinking or, more importantly, what he was *feeling*.

Dawson went and got her coat from the foyer closet. As he helped her into it, the concern on his face made her want to cry.

"I'm okay," she said, as she'd always told everyone after her mother had left...after Alan had left.

As if Dawson didn't believe her, he put his arms around her and gave her a hug that lasted a good long while. As he was holding her, she could feel the turmoil inside of him. He'd had his life turned upside down once before and now when he was starting to patch it back together again, she'd delivered a body blow that could shake up his world and his son's.

"I'm looking for another therapist for Luke. But I'd still like to see him on Monday," she said. "We're making progress. Considering his nightmare, I don't want to let up now. You and I... We'll just have to figure things out as we go."

He lifted her face and gave her a gentle kiss. As she drove home, she'd try to figure out if it was a kiss that meant goodbye.

Dawson dropped Luke off at Mikala's studio on Monday afternoon after school. When their gazes met, Mikala saw longing in his eyes. But they didn't have time to talk now. This was Luke's time.

Dawson waved to his son and managed a smile for Mikala. "I'll be back around five."

As Luke shed his coat and went into the music room, she focused on *him*...only on him. Once they were seated on the sofa, she said, "Tell me how your weekend went."

"I had an okay time with you and Dad Saturday," he said with a small smile.

She smiled back, trying to remember the camaraderie, the guitar playing, the feeling that she was part of a family, rather than what came after. "What about yesterday? Did Jake come over?"

"Yeah. He did. We played with my Wii and shot some hoops. He's not any better than I am." Luke stared down at the floor for a minute or two, then back at her. "Dad said he told you about my nightmare."

"Do *you* want to tell me about it?"

"Not really."

"Are you afraid if you talk about it, you'll have it again?"

He shrugged.

"It could be the opposite, you know. That if you talk about it, then maybe you won't have to have a nightmare about whatever it is again."

Luke seemed to think about that.

"If you don't feel like talking, we can do something else first. How about if you draw again to some music."

He considered her suggestion. "To my iPod shuffle?"

"No. This time I'd like you to draw to a CD *I* made. Would you consider that?"

"I guess. What kind of music?"

"A little bit of everything. Make yourself comfortable. I'm going to get my pad to take notes, and you tell me when you want to start."

Luke didn't take long. He kicked off his sneakers, poured the markers onto the table and opened the lid on the box of crayons.

"Ready," he announced with a half smile that reminded her of Dawson's.

She switched on the CD.

At first Luke's drawings were stream of consciousness scenery. There were trees, an elk, a house with a chimney with smoke coming out. The first piece of music was Tchaikovsky's *Swan Lake*. He was relaxed as he listened, drew easily, realistically, with suitable colors anyone would use.

The next selection was a recent pop hit. Luke's foot tapped with the music. He almost drew in rhythm with the song, first a kid dancing, then a man clapping. Maybe a dad?

They were going to have a lot to talk about. Luke obviously wanted his father's approval, whether he was playing basketball, doing math or ice skating. He wanted to do well so his dad would be proud. That was typical for a ten-year-old. The defiance and the fights didn't seem to click with his personality because Luke was a sweet kid. Was the anger stemming from the fact that his mom had died and he'd been with her when it had happened? Was he angry at himself because he hadn't been able to help her? Did he resent the fact that Dawson hadn't been there to protect him and his mom? They hadn't gotten into that yet. Their therapy hadn't gone that far.

Another selection played—Duke Ellington from another era. Luke didn't seem to react to it, just kept drawing small figures, larger ones, a boy and a man and an older man and a dog. No hidden secrets there. Luke wanted to be near his granddad again and she knew for certain he wanted a dog. Maybe now that he and Dawson were settled in the house that would be possible.

Mikala was lost in where she would go next with Luke, when she suddenly saw a change in his reaction. A popular country singer's ballad was playing.

Luke pressed so hard on the crayon in his hand that it broke. He stared at it, blinked a few times and then fixed his gaze straight ahead.

Mikala went on alert. Watching him closely, she saw him take the broken crayon and angrily draw a circle with legs—a table? His hand was shaking as he dropped the crayon. Suddenly he put both his hands to his face to cover it.

Mikala went over to the table and sat beside him while the country tune kept playing.

"Luke?"

When he looked at her, there were tears wetting his lashes, dripping down his cheeks. He didn't want her to see them, that was obvious. He was wiping them away as quickly as he could with the backs of his hands.

"Luke, it's all right. Tell me what's happening."

"It's the music! I *hate* that music," he yelled at her.

She went over to the CD player and turned it down—not off, just down. She wanted it low in the background to keep him in the memory because she was sure that's what was happening. He was remembering.

Sitting beside him again, a little closer this time, she asked, "Why don't you like the song?"

He shook his head, stared straight ahead, fingered the broken crayon and looked down at the paper. He just kept shaking his head as tears ran.

"What's going on, Luke? Can you tell me what's happening? What are you seeing?"

"We went Christmas shopping that day," he said, his voice breaking.

Mikala held her breath—she was afraid to interrupt the flow of memory.

"We went into a little store, and Mom bought a present for a friend. I asked her if we could get something for Dad for Christmas, but she said not now, not today. And she looked...funny." He glanced at the chart on the wall they'd used when he'd been trying to find the right word to describe his dad, then he stared at Mikala with the saddest eyes she'd ever seen. "She said we were having dinner with a friend before we went to our motel. His name was...Barry." Tears were coming again now and Luke couldn't seem to clear them to find his voice.

Mikala patted his hand so he'd know he wasn't alone. "What's upsetting you so much?"

"We went to a restaurant and country music was playing. That song played while we ate."

Luke caught his breath and a little hiccup escaped.

The words poured out as if a dam had burst and he couldn't keep them in. "I don't think Barry knew Mom was bringing me. They were kinda quiet. They didn't talk much when we ate. Barry asked me about school, what I liked to do, but he…he didn't really care. I could tell."

Children were so much more perceptive than adults gave them credit for. "How do you know he didn't care?"

"He just wanted to look at my mom. He just wanted to be *alone* with her. He didn't want me there."

"Did he say or do anything to make you think that?" All of Mikala's instincts were in high gear now and she had a terrible foreboding about what Luke was going to say next. His tears were muffling his voice, so she had to listen closely.

"Mom sent me for our coats. I gave the girl our tickets and she gave them to me right away. It didn't take long. Maybe Mom thought it would take longer. When I came back in— They were *kissing!*" He almost spat out the word as if it were the worst possible thing in the world he could have seen. "Mom saw me and she pulled away from Barry. He didn't look happy. She didn't look happy, either. They whispered something to each other and then we left."

"You and your mom."

He nodded and swiped at his nose.

Mikala handed him a tissue, but he just balled it up and held it in his fist. "She didn't talk right away. She looked…looked funny and she was holding the steering wheel really tight. Snow was falling when we were driving. We couldn't see through it. But I had to know— I asked her why she'd kissed him. I told her she shouldn't be kissing anybody but *Dad.* That's when she started crying. She told me she loved me, but she said she loved Barry, too. She said tomorrow she was taking me back to Dad and moving out of the house. But she'd come back and see me. And I could visit her." Luke shook his head, reliving it. "I didn't want her to move out! I told her she couldn't go. That's when...that's when the car slid on the ice and we went off the road. We rolled over and then we banged into a tree. She called my name and I tried calling to her but then...but then— I don't remember anything else, not until I woke up in the hospital and Dad was there."

Without hesitation Mikala put her arms around Luke and held him as he cried, seeing the scene in her own mind as he described it, reliving the conversation in the car with him. Kelly probably hadn't fastened her seat belt because she was distracted...upset about what she was doing...leaving her son.

Luke mumbled against her neck, "It was my fault. It was all *my* fault."

Her protest was vehement and firm. "No, Luke. It was *not.*"

But Luke didn't seem to hear her. "Dad's going to hate me. He is. He's going to be so mad at Mom. I can't tell him. *I can't.*"

Slowly Mikala pulled away from the ten-year-old, took a tissue and helped wipe his tears. She loved this little boy...was beginning to love him as if he were her own. She'd tried to keep her distance but that had been so hard to do. Now she had to convince him that none of this was his fault. But she might need Dawson's help with that.

"Luke, sometimes grown-ups make decisions that

hurt other people. Your mom made a decision that was going to hurt you and your dad. But that's not *your* fault. She was the adult and she was driving. *You* didn't cause the accident. I think you really need to tell your dad what happened. If you keep secrets, he'll know something's wrong. You want to stay close to him, don't you?"

Luke sniffed, swiped at his nose with the tissue, and then nodded.

"I know your dad, and I know he won't be angry with *you.* Will you let me call him so he can come here and help you, too?"

"You want me to tell him now?"

"Yes, I do. And if you need help, I'll be right here." Now was the time. She was sure of it. A memory like this would be awful for Luke to carry.

She let Luke think about it for a while, and then he nodded.

"Okay."

Mikala didn't tell Dawson much on the phone, just that she thought it would be best if he would come join their session. He came immediately. When he saw his son, his bedraggled appearance with tear-stained cheeks, his woebegone expression, Dawson looked to Mikala for an explanation.

She said, "Luke remembered what happened the day of the accident. I think it's best if he tells you about it, but I'll help him if he can't. Right, Luke?"

Luke nodded, but looked fearful.

With Mikala on one side of him and his dad on the other, Luke told Dawson the same thing he'd told Mikala and began crying all over again. Dawson kept his arm around his son, brought him into his shoulder, squeezed him tight.

Hurting for both of them, Mikala could see Dawson's pain, feel the sense of betrayal that went so deep he couldn't look at her.

Yet he kept telling Luke, "It's not your fault. None of it is your fault. We're okay. You and I are okay."

Dawson held on to Luke as long as Luke needed to be held. In that time when father and son bonded so deeply, Mikala was happy for them. But she also understood in her soul that her hopes for a future with Dawson were dashed. How would he be able to get beyond his wife's affair? Because that's what it had obviously been. She'd been prepared to leave him for another man. What would that betrayal do to Dawson's sense of pride? To his sense of trust? To Mikala's chance at a relationship with him?

When Luke's tears stopped, Dawson looked as if he'd been through a war. "I know we should talk," he said to Mikala, "but I don't want to leave him right now."

"Of course you don't. You need some quiet time. He needs to let the rest of it come out, if there is any more.

"Luke…" she said, gently touching his shoulder. She wasn't going to talk about him as if he weren't there. "If you remember anything else, it's okay to tell your dad. And you can call *me* if you want to, anytime."

Luke slipped his hand into Dawson's. "I'll tell Dad."

"That's the way it should be." Father and son could face the world together now in a new way.

Dawson held on to Luke, but his gaze locked on to Mikala's as he opened the door.

Her heart broke for Dawson and what he must be

feeling, and she ached for Luke. He'd remembered his mother was going to desert him. She so knew how *that* felt. Luke and Dawson were going to have a tough night, but they had each other and that's what mattered.

As she stood in the doorway and watched them walk away, she put her hand on her stomach. She might not have Dawson, but she had her baby. That's what had to matter to her most now.

Chapter Twelve

Forty-eight hours later Mikala waved goodbye to her last client of the day, watching as mother and daughter climbed into their van in the B and B's parking lot. She was fine as long as she was working. But at night, and at every moment in between when her thoughts roamed, she thought only about Dawson and Luke. She could call them and yet…

If they needed her help, they'd call. Wouldn't they? Besides, Luke had another appointment tomorrow.

She was about to turn away and go back inside when she saw Dawson's SUV pull into the slot the van had vacated. Her heart heaved a sigh of relief…but then it tripped fast. They still had so much to discuss.

He was dressed casually in a sweater and jeans and hadn't bothered with a coat. She had to wonder if this had been an impulsive decision to come see her.

He was at the door before she noticed the manila envelope in his hand. What was that about?

He attempted a small smile and she attempted one back. "Is this a bad time?" he asked.

"No. It's fine. How's Luke?"

"I'm not sure. I think he's still blaming himself. But I'm hoping you can help him with that. I keep telling him he was eight years old. There's nothing he could have done that would have changed anything. But there's still a gap between us, and I don't know if he believes me. When you see him tomorrow, you'll get a better gauge on that. I didn't come to talk about Luke, though."

She backed up a few steps and gestured him inside. They went over to the love seat and sat. Yet she didn't feel close to Dawson. It wasn't simply the six inches between them, but it was in his posture and the way he leaned away rather than toward her. His green eyes were so serious she started to get very scared.

He handed her the envelope. "This is for you. There's information in there about two bank accounts I've opened. One is for you to use now for whatever you need. The other is for our child's education. All you have to do is go to Miners Bluff Community Bank and sign the papers."

Mikala's breath left her lungs. Her heart seemed to fall to her toes. What Dawson had learned about his wife had changed *everything* between them. Everything but her feelings toward him. Those were stronger than ever. But Dawson...

She could see the turmoil in his eyes, feel the tension stringing his body. He was having trouble accepting all of it, as much as Luke was. Still, she was hurt that he thought money would solve anything.

She handed him back the envelope. "I don't want your money."

"I know you're independent, Mikala, but you have to be practical."

"Oh, I *am* being practical. Your money won't take your place if I raise our child alone."

"That's a low blow, especially right now." He looked disappointed in her and hurt himself.

"I didn't mean it that way. But can't you see? Didn't you learn anything from what happened in your marriage?"

There was an impatient edge to his voice. "My marriage has nothing to do with this. You and I were both careless and now we have the consequences to deal with."

"Your marriage has *everything* to do with this," she protested. "You wanted to give Kelly and Luke material possessions. But what they needed was *you*—your presence, your caring and your attention."

"I didn't confide in you, Mikala, to have you turn it all around on me!" He looked angry now, and she knew anger was easier. He wouldn't have to deal with deeper emotions that were tearing him up inside.

"I admit I should have spent more time at home," he said with regret. "But I was doing what I thought a man should do. *Provide.*"

"Provide what, Dawson? Yes, a roof over their heads, clothes and the necessities. But were you thinking about providing when you wanted to make your business a success? When you worked sixteen-hour days to get more contracts? Was that about your family or was it about *you* wanting to succeed?"

He stood and slammed the manila envelope on her desk. "If I didn't succeed, men would be out of work and we wouldn't have had a financial future. You talk about success with such disdain. But you want to succeed, too. You're a perfectionist, Mikala, just as much as I am. What life do *you* have outside of your work?"

"I was trying to build one," she said, staring at him pointedly. "But I realize now, *you* weren't. You were looking for an escape and I was it. How I could have been so foolish yet again, I don't know. Just take your papers and leave."

"The papers stay. If you tear them up, I'll give you another set. I went to the bank and I set these up because I need some time to figure this all out. I married Kelly *because* she was pregnant. And she got pregnant on purpose so I *would* marry her."

Dawson's revelation stunned Mikala. "You never told me that."

"Why would I? On one hand I'd looked at it that she'd loved me so much she became pregnant with my child. But on the other, I felt manipulated. We were three years into our marriage when I found out and I was determined to make our marriage work for Luke's sake."

"But you didn't," Mikala murmured.

"No. I absolutely went about it all wrong. My father's bankruptcy destroyed his marriage. I was going to make damn sure that didn't happen to me!"

The heavy silence let Dawson's words echo over and over again. At his vehement explanation of feelings,

Mikala doubted if even he had realized his motive for working so much before now.

"Look, Mikala. You might think you don't want the money, but right now I can't offer you more. I just found out my wife betrayed me. How do you think I'd be ready to jump into anything else?"

"You said you grew apart. Did you really *not* know?"

She wasn't trying to hurt Dawson more. She was trying to make him see that sometimes being blind was easier than facing the truth. *She'd* been blind about their involvement because she'd loved him. Maybe she'd always loved him, and that had kept her from realizing his feelings weren't that deep. And now she was pregnant with his child and she had to make decisions, too.

"Maybe I was blind," Dawson admitted. "But I wasn't looking for signs that Kelly was having an affair. She gave me no reason to doubt her."

No reason? Mikala couldn't believe that. Especially when a man and woman were intimate, they usually knew.

As she stared at Dawson, he realized her underlying message. His cheeks flushed a little. He moved away from her toward the door. "I'm not going to say something I'll regret."

She got her bearings, considered her abilities, her options, Luke's and Dawson's. And she considered what was best for Luke, just as Dawson always had. "I found two therapists in Flagstaff who might be good with Luke. They're play therapists, not music therapists, but I've examined the way they work and I think Luke could relate. I think he and I need at least a few sessions to tie up everything we've stirred up. I can be objective about Luke, Dawson. And I think I can be objective about you, too, whether you believe that or not."

He gave her a look that went straight to her heart. "You can't be objective about this any more than I can. I'll see you tomorrow."

When Dawson left her studio, Mikala stared at the manila envelope on her desk and began to cry.

Two weeks later Mikala put a pan of banana bread in the oven as her aunt busily prepared a few salads for guests who would be arriving later in the afternoon.

Anna said, "I saw Dawson's car last night. I guess Luke had an appointment."

Mikala didn't say anything. Her aunt knew she couldn't talk about a client, even if it was Dawson and his son. Her heart was so heavy. Yet at the same time she knew her baby was growing inside of her. She knew Luke was finally processing his memories and dealing with them. He and Dawson seemed to be talking at home, too, from what Luke had told her.

"It didn't look as if you and Dawson talked at all. He and Luke seemed to leave in a hurry."

No, she and Dawson weren't talking. He'd dropped off Luke and then picked him up. End of story.

"Oh, I know you can't talk about it," Aunt Anna said. "And you've been doing admirably, considering the circumstances."

That made Mikala stare at her aunt. "What circumstances?"

"Your pregnancy."

Mikala felt her mouth drop and emotion come into

her throat. Talking around the lump, she asked, "How could you possibly know?"

"Mikala Conti, I raised you. I've lived with you all these years. Do you think I can't tell when you're pale in the morning? When you don't eat breakfast? Do you think I haven't seen you turn green when I put clam chowder in front of you? Your mother couldn't handle seafood, either. That was a dead giveaway."

Mikala went to the table and pulled out a chair. She had a feeling this was going to be a long heart-to-heart, at least for as long as the bread baked. "I want this baby. I love it already. The doctor says everything looks fine and I've already started prenatal care."

"And Dawson?"

"You know I can't tell you what's happening there."

"You can tell me if he wants his baby."

"He wants to *pay* for his baby. He wants to start a college fund for his baby. I don't know if he's actually realized I have a tiny life inside of here." She patted her midriff. "He's dealing with a lot, Aunt Anna. And involving himself in another committed relationship, especially with a woman who's pregnant, just wasn't part of his plan."

"Love isn't part of anyone's plan, I don't think," her aunt said with that knowing look that somehow always gave Mikala comfort. "Do you know what I think?"

Mikala was almost afraid to ask. "Whether I want to know or not, you're going to tell me anyway, aren't you?"

Her aunt grinned. "You bet I am. The dance at the Mayfield Mansion is coming up next weekend."

The Mayfield Mansion was part of an estate set aside to preserve Miners Bluff history. Every year a fundraising dance was held there to defer some of the cost of keeping it open to tourists. Mikala had attended many of the dances, but this year—

"I don't feel like dancing," she told her aunt.

"But that's the whole point! You need to buck up. Enjoy the news of that little one growing inside of you. Celebrate your life just the way it is, whether Dawson's in it or not. Don't you think?"

Celebrate her life just the way it was. She loved Dawson. She also loved Luke. And whether or not that love was returned, love was always a good thing. The little life growing inside of her was going to direct her future. And, yes, she was looking forward to that. She couldn't wait for the diapers, and the pacifiers and even the sleepless nights. She couldn't wait for seeing her child walk, ride a tricycle, go to preschool. There was so very much to look forward to, no matter what part Dawson played in her life. And if she just kept loving him, maybe someday—

"I'd have to go shopping."

"Maybe, maybe not. I happen to have a gown I wore to the winter festival many, many years ago…when I was first in love with Silas."

"First in love?" Mikala asked. They hadn't really talked about this.

"Oh, I do love him all over again. And I think he loves me. We're figuring it out. But in the meantime, I have this beautiful sapphire-blue velvet dress in my closet that can easily be altered to fit you."

"Are *you* going to the dance?"

"I certainly am. Silas invited me to go with him. I wouldn't miss it. Silas is even going to wear his Western tux. That will be a sight."

Her aunt and Silas Decker in love *would* be a sight.

Mikala knew she had to put her relationship with Dawson on hold. She had to figure out what happened next for her and her baby. Going to the dance at the Mayfield Mansion could be the first step.

Dawson aimed at the backboard over the garage and landed a hook shot. Passing the basketball to Luke, he watched his son aim carefully, then toss the ball with all his might. It rolled around the rim, then dropped in. Luke ran and caught the ball.

"Do you want to take a break?" Dawson asked his son.

"Sure, if you need it, Dad." Luke grinned.

He'd been grinning and talking more each day. His son was healing...thanks to Mikala.

Luke looked around as if he was assessing the yard, the house and their life. Then he said, "Mikala would like it out here. She might even like to play basketball. We should ask her over again." He gave his dad a sideways glance to see how he'd received the suggestion.

Ever since the day he'd taken the bank information to Mikala, Dawson's insides had been churning, his heart aching, his mind going over everything he and Mikala had said. His marriage had been long over *before* the night of Kelly's accident, and he'd been so determined to keep them together that he hadn't faced it. He hadn't wanted to fail. He hadn't wanted *his* marriage to end up like his parents' marriage had. Yet it had, anyway. Two people, separate instead of together. Two people, who maybe didn't belong together in the first place, but stayed together because of their lifestyle and their son.

Only… Kelly had been ready to walk out. Kelly had betrayed him. Kelly had fallen in love with another man.

Dawson was still processing everything that had happened, still trying to figure out each mistake he'd made, what he could have done differently.

And in the midst of all of it, he ached for Mikala. He ached for the baby she was going to have. *Their* baby. Could he be a good father this time around? Would she even consider letting him back into her life after his reaction to her pregnancy…his reaction to committing to her…his silence since then?

Luke was watching his dad carefully now. He revealed, "Aunt Anna told me Mikala grew up with her. When I asked why, Aunt Anna said Mikala's mom left when she was little. She didn't really want to *be* a mom. Maybe my mom didn't want to be a mom anymore. Mikala says that's not true. What do *you* think?"

Wow. Now that he and Luke were communicating, he wished he was wiser and knew exactly what to say. But he let his heart guide him.

"I believe your mom loved you very much. I think she stopped loving me because I wasn't the best husband or dad I could be. But she *never* stopped loving you."

"But she was going to *leave*."

"I know." That knowledge lanced Dawson deeply. All he could do was listen and acknowledge Luke's pain, too.

Dawson remained silent, unsure what to say. He was totally unprepared for what came next.

Luke bounced his basketball a few times, casting a quick look at Dawson. "You know, Dad, I like Mikala a lot. And…if she ever married someone, she would *never* leave her kid. Because she knows how it feels. Right?"

Luke had apparently been doing a lot of thinking since his memory returned. "Right," Dawson answered, knowing it was true. He repeated, "Marry someone?"

"Marry *us*," Luke murmured. Then seeing his father didn't have an unfavorable reaction, he asked, "Don't you really, *really* like her? I do."

This question of Luke's definitely required an answer—one he could give wholeheartedly. "Yes, I really, really like her."

And with sudden shining clarity, he knew he *more* than liked her…more than desired her. He loved Mikala Conti. Yes, he did. He *loved* her. Mikala was honest and loyal and would love their child until her dying day. Maybe him, too, if he'd give her a chance…give *them* a chance.

He might have ruined everything. If she'd felt anything deeply for him, he might have spoiled it. That last time they'd made love, Mikala had finally let her guard down with him, and he hadn't cherished that fact as he should have. He hadn't cherished her and their baby as he should have.

The turmoil that had stolen his sleep as well as his appetite suddenly ceased. He saw that Luke could accept Mikala as he couldn't accept any other woman… that she'd be a mother he could trust…that she'd be a wife Dawson could trust. He understood the mistakes he'd made and would not repeat them. He finally removed his blinders and saw clearly that he wanted a life—and a family—with Mikala. She was his future. Now he just had to convince her that he was hers.

Chapter Thirteen

The Mayfield Mansion was absolutely beautiful. Mikala tried to concentrate on the polished old wood, the crown molding, the antique furniture, as she moved from room to room, talking with Celeste and Clay, Jenny and Zack, Katie, Riley and Noah. There were some new faces, men she hadn't seen before, and they looked at her with interest. She felt pretty tonight in her aunt's beautiful dress. The sapphire-blue velvet swept her ankles; the off-the-shoulder neck and long sleeves hugged her closely. The waist was tightly fitted before it swept out into a full skirt, and she was very aware that a few months from now she wouldn't be able to fasten the tiny buttons down the back of the dress. With it she'd worn Dawson's necklace. She never took it off. The charm holder with its piano charm was a talisman she'd always cherish.

Music was playing in the grand ballroom. She

headed that way, even though she didn't intend to stay long. Immediately she spotted Silas and her Aunt Anna waltzing as if they were made to dance together. Jenny and Zack were dancing now, too, as well as Celeste and Clay. If only—

Suddenly her breath caught. Dawson was there, striding across the room toward her. Her heart fluttered and for a moment she thought of running in the other direction. She felt so much, and she couldn't just have a casual conversation tonight as if her heart didn't still feel trampled. But he'd seen her now. And unlike their brief encounters when he came and went with Luke, there was a new look of determination in his eyes that told her he'd come after her if she ran! Because he was ready to talk about the baby again? About the bank account she wouldn't sign her name to?

As he approached, she noticed everything about him. He was dressed in a Western-cut suit with a white shirt and a black bolo tie, with a horseshoe holding it around his neck. He looked so good she wanted to cry.

But she wouldn't. Except in her bedroom at night when she let her tears fall, she'd held her emotions together. Her pride was all she had left with Dawson, and she wouldn't let it disintegrate around her. She straightened her back, raised her chin a little higher and waited for him.

When he stood in front of her, he held out his hand. "Dance with me?"

"Dawson—" In his arms again, how could she hold in all she was feeling?

"Dance with me, Mikala."

There was an insistence in his voice that she couldn't refuse. She nodded.

As he took her into his arms, she asked softly, "Where's Luke tonight?"

"Dad's visiting. They're having a guys' night."

Dawson's arm wrapped around her, and she was transported back to the first time they'd danced at their senior prom, the next time at their reunion, and then two months ago at Zack and Jenny's party. Every time she'd danced with Dawson they'd become a little closer. And tonight...

He pulled her tighter and when she gazed up into his eyes she saw, what? Emotion, that was for sure. But about what? How she was helping Luke? About everything that had happened? Regrets he might want to talk about?

In spite of all her questions, she got lost in the music and the dance and Dawson. They moved together as if they'd been doing it forever. Her blood heated, her face flushed, her body molded to his.

When the song ended, Dawson tucked her hand into the crook of his arm. "Come with me."

There were French doors leading to a balcony. He opened one, guided her through and then closed the door behind them. A winter chill still nipped the air, but there was a hint of spring lingering there, too... new life beginning to bud.

When she turned to Dawson, he took both of her hands into his. Panic somersaulted in her stomach. What if he was going to move away from Miners Bluff and go back to Phoenix with Luke? What if—

"Stop thinking," he ordered gently. "Just look at me and listen. Okay?"

"I'll listen," she said shakily, not sure she wanted to.

"I always thought you were the prettiest, kindest

girl I'd ever met. I made so many mistakes since I arrived here—with Luke and with you. But thanks to you, Luke and I are really becoming father and son again. Mikala, you've given me my son back and I will always be grateful for that."

If this was about gratitude—

"Stop thinking," he ordered again gently with a smile that warmed her all over. "Yes, I'm grateful. But I'm so much more. I've realized I fell for you in high school, only you never knew that. I fell for you all over again at the reunion, but denied it. How could I feel anything when I had so much going on with Luke? But as each day went by, it was harder and harder to deny those feelings. Luke and I are on the same page now about a lot of things. And we're in total agreement about something very important—we both want you to be part of our family."

To Mikala's complete astonishment, Dawson dropped to one knee, pulled a ring from his pocket and took her hand. "Mikala, I want you to know straight out this proposal has *nothing* to do with your pregnancy...*our* pregnancy. My proposal is all about wanting to spend the rest of my life with *you*. Will you marry me?"

Speechless, Mikala was overcome with emotion. She could see the sincerity in Dawson's eyes, the honesty in his expression, the love all over his face. With him looking at her like that, her pride meant nothing.

Only her true feelings for him mattered, and she had to tell him what they were. "I love you, Dawson Barrett. I can't wait to be a mom to our baby, *and* to Luke, if you'll let me."

Dawson slipped the heart-shaped diamond onto her

finger, then stood and took her into his arms. "You will be the best mom a child could ever have. And I will work hard to be the husband you've always dreamed of. Forever."

His kiss was everything she'd dreamed a kiss could be. He swept her away with it—into his heart, into his life, into their future.

Suddenly the French doors opened and she heard applause. Dawson's lips clung to hers for a moment and then he leaned back and laughed, his arm encircling her, keeping her close. All of their friends were standing there, watching, smiling and applauding.

"Way to go," Riley called.

"Congratulations, boy!" Silas said.

Dawson murmured in Mikala's ear, "I think our friends approve."

"I know *I* do." Mikala's eyes filled with tears of happiness.

Dawson bent his head and kissed her again.

Epilogue

Mikala heard the strumming of a guitar and headed toward the nursery.

It was still early on in her pregnancy. The morning after the dance she and Dawson had told Luke he would have a brother or sister. Looking from one of them to the other, he'd asked, "When are you getting married?" as if he'd known all along they would be. So after more discussions with Luke, deciding stability was important for all of them now, she and Dawson had married in a quiet ceremony in the backyard with Dawson's dad, Aunt Anna, Silas and their friends. Celeste and Jenny had been her attendants with little Abby as her flower girl and Luke the ring bearer.

That had been two weeks ago. Yesterday the furniture had been delivered for the nursery. They'd wanted

Luke to be part of the planning of the baby's room and he'd entered into it wholeheartedly, helping them paint the walls a pale yellow, insisting his brother or sister should have little ducks on the coverlet on the crib. The room was as bright as her future with Dawson and she was so in love she couldn't see straight.

Luke had asked her to give him guitar lessons and she'd happily begun doing that, transitioning from therapy into music lessons. Now, as she entered the baby's room, she found him sitting in the glider-rocker they'd bought, with its pink-and-blue-plaid cushions, strumming the chords she'd taught him. He had a piece of paper on his knee and was trying to juggle the junior guitar and stare at it at the same time.

"What's up?" she asked, looking at the boy who was so much like his dad.

He rested the neck of the guitar against his shoulder. "I'm practicing."

"Practicing for what?"

"A lullaby. When my brother or sister comes in November, I'll be ready."

Mikala laughed, went over to him and gave him a hug, guitar and all. "You're going to be the best brother."

"I second that," Dawson's deep male baritone said from the doorway.

When Mikala looked at her new husband, joy and excitement overtook her.

He seemed to sense that as he crossed the room to her. "Now that we've decorated the nursery, and Luke's practicing a lullaby, we have something even more important to do."

"What's that?" Luke asked, echoing Mikala's thoughts.

"We have to pick out names."

"I can look on the computer," Luke said enthusiastically.

"That's a great idea," Dawson agreed.

"I'll do it now and practice later." Carefully lifting his guitar, he hurried from the room to do something very important.

"Do you have any favorite names in mind?" Dawson asked Mikala as he took her into his arms.

"I'm open to whatever we all like."

"And are you open to a night of unbridled passion?" he asked as he teased her neck with several wet kisses.

She laughed. "I don't know how unbridled it can be without having a soundproof bedroom," she whispered back in a low voice.

"I have a surprise for you." He took a brochure from his jeans pocket and handed it to her.

She unfolded it and found a beautiful Sedona resort. "Dawson, it looks magnificent. Those red rocks, blue sky, a spa."

"Dad can come up and stay with Luke next weekend. Two nights and three days of a honeymoon with you. Can you make room in your schedule?"

Mikala wrapped her arms around his neck. "On second thought, I don't think I'll have time for the spa. Not if we're giving massages to each other."

Laughing, Dawson swung her around. Then he set her down, looked lovingly into her eyes and said simply, "You've made me the happiest man in the world. You know that, don't you?"

She brushed his hair from his forehead and smiled

with a happily-ever-after song in her heart. "I feel the same."

Dawson's kiss was a renewal of the vows they'd so recently professed. His kiss promised to make all of her dreams come true.

* * * * *

Don't miss Riley O'Rourke's story,
RILEY'S BABY BOY,
the next installment in Karen Rose Smith's
miniseries REUNION BRIDES!
On sale August 2012,
wherever Harlequin books are sold.

COMING NEXT MONTH from Harlequin®
Special Edition®
AVAILABLE JULY 24, 2012

#2203 PUPPY LOVE IN THUNDER CANYON
Montana Mavericks: Back in the Saddle
Christyne Butler
An intense, aloof surgeon meets his match in a friendly librarian who believes that emotional connections can heal—and she soon teaches him that love is the best medicine!

#2204 THE DOCTOR AND THE SINGLE MOM
Men of Mercy Medical
Teresa Southwick
Dr. Adam Stone picked the wrong place to rent. Or maybe just the wrong lady to rent from. Jill Beck is beloved—and protected—by the entire town. One wrong move with the sexy single mom could cost him a career in Blackwater Lake, Montana—and the chance to fill up the empty place inside him.

#2205 RILEY'S BABY BOY
Reunion Brides
Karen Rose Smith
Feuding families make a surpise baby and even bigger challenges. Are Brenna McDougall and Riley O'Rourke ready for everything life has in store for them? Including a little surpise romance?

#2206 HIS BEST FRIEND'S WIFE
Gina Wilkins
How much is widowed mom Renae Sanchez willing to risk for a sexy, secretive man from her past...a man she once blamed for her husband's death?

#2207 A WEEK TILL THE WEDDING
Linda Winstead Jones
Jacob Tasker and Daisy Bell think they are doing the right thing when they pretend to still be engaged for the sake of his sick grandmother. But as their fake nuptials start leading to real love, they find out that granny may have a few tricks up her old sleeve!

#2208 ONE IN A BILLION
Home to Harbor Town
Beth Kery
A potential heiress—the secret baby of her mother's affair—is forced by the will to work with her nemesis, a sexy tycoon, to figure out the truth about her paternity, and what it means for the company of which she now owns half!

You can find more information on upcoming Harlequin® titles, free excerpts and more at www.HarlequinInsideRomance.com.

HSECNM0712

Angie Bartlett and Michael Robinson are friends. And following the death of his wife, Angie's best friend, their bond has grown even more. But that's all there is...right?

Read on for an exciting excerpt of WITHIN REACH by Sarah Mayberry, available August 2012 from Harlequin® Superromance®.

"HEY. RIGHT ON TIME," Michael said as he opened the door.

The first thing Angie registered was his fresh haircut and that he was clean shaven—a significant change from the last time she'd visited. Then her gaze dropped to his broad chest and the skintight black running pants molded to his muscular legs. The words died on her lips and she blinked, momentarily stunned by her acute awareness of him.

"You've cut your hair," she said stupidly.

"Yeah. Decided it was time to stop doing my caveman impersonation."

He gestured for her to enter. As she brushed past him she caught the scent of his spicy deodorant. He preceded her to the kitchen and her gaze traveled across his shoulders before dropping to his backside. Angie had always made a point of not noticing Michael's body. They were friends and she didn't want to know that kind of stuff. Now, however, she was forcibly reminded that he was a *very* attractive man.

Suddenly she didn't know where to look.

It was then that she noticed the other changes—the clean kitchen, the polished dining table and the living room free of clutter and abandoned clothes.

"Look at you go." Surely these efforts meant he was rejoining life.

HSREXP0812

He shrugged, but seemed pleased she'd noticed. "Getting there."

They maintained eye contact and the moment expanded. A connection that went beyond the boundaries of their friendship formed between them. Suddenly Angie wanted Michael in ways she'd never felt before. *Ever.*

"Okay. Let's get this show on the road," his six-year-old daughter, Eva, announced as she marched into the room.

Angie shook her head to break the spell and focused on Eva. "Great. Looking forward to a little light shopping?"

"Yes!" Eva gave a squeal of delight, then kissed her father goodbye.

Angie didn't feel 100 percent comfortable until she was sliding into the driver's seat.

Which was dumb. It was nothing. A stupid, odd bit of awareness that meant *nothing.* Michael was still Michael, even if he was gorgeous. Just because she'd tuned in to that fact for a few seconds didn't change anything.

Does Angie's new awareness mark a permanent shift in their relationship? Find out in WITHIN REACH by Sarah Mayberry, available August 2012 from Harlequin® Superromance®.